WITHDR

Date D

BIRDS OF WINTER

BIRDS OF WINTER

Theodore Vrettos

BOSTON
Houghton Mifflin Company
1980

Library of Congress Cataloging in Publication Data

Vrettos, Theodore.
  Birds of winter.

  I. Title.
PZ4.V97Bi [PS3572.R38] 813'.54 80-11942
ISBN 0-395-29455-X

Printed in the United States of America

P 10 9 8 7 6 5 4 3 2 1

To Vas

φιλῶ σε

ONE

From the open window of the bedroom Jason fixed his eyes on the thin peninsula extending toward Taenarus, the entrance into Hades. His father's olive trees struggled for life on that carcass of volcanic earth. Under its parched skin his grandfather slept. *My little Icarus, there is no other sun like the sun of Greece. He is a worker of miracles. He takes the heavy beads of dew that slumber on these olive leaves and with one majestic touch resurrects them into eternity.*

Grandfather Andreas, spinner of songs and legends, high priest of a wretched land that could nourish only the humble olive tree, the emaciated goat, a place where nothing survived but the spirit of a decaying past.

Jason slowly came away from the window and sat once more beside the bed. His mother was at the core of pain. She crumpled one corner of the sheet in her hand and began twisting and pulling it until the veins of her arm swelled and turned blue. "Help me, little Virgin," she murmured. "Please help me!"

The smells of birth suffocated him. He was deafened by the bells of Saint Chrysostomos. *Hollow cries to a dying God!* Christ was yet unrisen on this Great Friday of Easter Week but already Livani had come to life, old women sauntering dourly through the narrow streets of the village, black shawls thrown over their heads, crossing themselves with each peal of the bell; the men propped back in their chairs outside the taverna, sipping coffee or wine, smoking, arguing with their hands; and the children, unaware of Christ's agony, playing among the tall cypresses that guarded the schoolyard. The day was warm and saturated with the scent of jasmine.

"Help me, little Virgin!"

Jason felt a cold gush of air. He looked up and saw his father charging into the bedroom, hands caked with dirt, fiery eyes inquiring.

Jason shook his head.

"Are you blind?" cried his father. "Her hour has come. Go summon the midwife."

Under his breath Jason vomited the words, "Summon her yourself, you horny bastard!" He slammed the kitchen door shut and hurried into the yard. When he reached the street he started to run and did not stop until he approached the church. A handful of women was assembled on the steps, their necks craned toward the funereal words drifting out from the open door:

> *Sweet Child of God,*
> *We mourn Your death today,*
> *As Joseph of Arimathea*
> *Takes You down from the accursed tree,*
> *And the women anoint You with myrrh ...*

Words long buried in his childhood, faded memories of dead Easter Weeks, fasting forty whole days, denying himself every comfort for that supreme moment when the priest would slide open the Beautiful Door of the altar and proclaim to the world that Christ was Risen, a moment when evil was miraculously transformed into virtue, when faces glowed and hearts spilled with love.

The midwife's house was newly whitened for Easter. For as long as Jason could remember, the same debilitated staircase clung to its side. He climbed the steps carefully and knocked on the door. It opened a crack then slammed shut. He heard the midwife shout, "Go away. I am not dressed!"

"Kyra Maria, my mother's hour has come!"

"Is that you, Jason?"

"Please open the door."

The midwife let him in. "Are you absolutely certain about your mother?" she rasped.

"Yes."

Hastily she buttoned the bodice of her black dress with her thick coarse fingers. "But I was just about to go to church."

"You must hurry. She is in great pain."

Kyra Maria retreated into her bedroom, leaving the door wide open. She had trouble with the hem of her dress. It was stuck against her hips but after a few desperate pulls she released it and began combing her long black hair, bringing it around until it formed a large bun behind her head. Stepping before a small mirror, she began smoothing down a few strands of gray hair that were jutting out near the temple. "A fine Resurrection this is going to be!"

He implored her to hurry.

"Christ is not crucified every day!" she exclaimed. With exasperation she gave up on the unruly gray hair then stooped under the bed and dragged out an old canvas bag. The floor shook when she returned to the kitchen. Carefully she took out some of the contents from the bag and examined them: a bottle of iodine, a thick package of cotton, several rolls of gauze, many bottles of various sizes with hand-written labels, some adhesive tape, scissors, more small bottles, and an odd-looking instrument with rubber handles. She put everything into the bag, handed it to Jason, then followed him out of the kitchen and down the perilous steps.

By this time the sun was making one final attempt to vault over Taygetus, fearful of the tragedy that the night would bring: the wailing cries of death, the tears, the mournful preparation for Christ's entombment.

The streets were now filled with people. Any moment Pappa Sotiri would lift the heavy wooden cross with Christ

5

nailed to it, carry it out of the church, through the converging faithful of Livani, and past the latticed canopy of the taverna where clusters of old men sat—sour, bitter, dried-up bones. They went there every morning, pulled their chairs close to the window, and measured each passing face, each skirt and bare leg. Their greatest target was Kyra Maria's idiot son Fanoulis, whose turtle mind could not keep pace with his twenty-eight years.

Is this to be my life, Grandfather Andreas, this detestable village where the right hand watches the left, where the very hairs of my head are counted every day?

He lost his patience with the midwife. She had tarried far behind and was now leaning against the door of the bakery, wiping her brow. He called out to her and when she made no response he went back and offered his hand but she pushed it away. "There was a time when I flew over these streets. My skin was the color of honey; my blood boiled with youth!"

He proceeded a few paces then looked back and saw her trudging toward him, still mumbling and rolling her head. When they entered the yard he noticed his father pacing furiously on the porch. Marko rushed toward them, grabbed Kyra Maria's arm, and yanked her into the house. She rebelled, crying, "Marko, I cannot work this way. I must rest for a moment."

He refused to listen. Jason could not cope with his wrath. He edged past his father and the midwife, and made his way into the bedroom. His mother's face was pale, her groans filled the house. Suddenly the midwife shoved him away and took hold of his mother's wrist. She studied the swollen belly then turned and snarled at Marko, "I warned you to keep that thing away from Katina!"

Jason walked to the window.

"For years I have warned you . . ."

There was a soft knock on the kitchen door. His aunt Yianoula showed her face, her thick black eyebrows, hair on

6

upper lip. "I would have come sooner," she puffed, "but Renio is not feeling well."

"What are you doing here?" Kyra Maria exclaimed.

"I came to help."

The midwife snorted. "You faint at a drop of blood!" She moved away from the bed and glared at them. "Why are you all standing there with your arms folded? I need hot water and clean cloths. In the name of the Virgin, do you think a woman simply spreads open her legs and out it comes, pffft?"

Yianoula raced into the kitchen and came back with the cloths. Marko brought in the large white kettle of steaming water. They placed everything on the small table while Kyra Maria went after her canvas bag. As soon as she returned, she signaled to Marko and he emptied some water into a white basin. Yianoula took the midwife's hands and slowly dipped them into the water, scrubbing them thoroughly with a cake of hard soap. "A good birth," she stammered.

"Health to your hands," said Marko, lips quivering.

The midwife dried her hands on a towel. "Leave the room—all of you. I have much work before me."

•   •

Night fell. The wind calmed itself. Unable to stay in the house, Jason stepped outside. The yard was dark. Stars were straining in the sky, trying to reach their full stature. He wandered as far as the south grove then slowly returned to the yard and sat on the porch for a while before going into the house. Yianoula was cooking lentil soup.

"Where is my father?" he asked.

"In the bedroom."

He seated himself at the table in deep thought. Yianoula put a bowl of soup in front of him but he pushed it away. "I am not hungry," he said. She paid no attention to him. She cut two thick slices of dark bread and placed them next to the bowl of soup.

7

"I told you, I am not hungry!"

He heard the off-key strains of a chant drifting in from the yard. After a few moments, Yianoula's husband sauntered into the kitchen, a thirty-eight-year-old jester with spirited eyes and restless heart. Byzantium resurrected in a regal posture, powerful shoulders over a wiry frame, raven mustache and hair, he held a lit taper in his hand and was chanting, "Christ is Risen from the dead—ne, ti, ri, rem!"

"Pavlo, stop it!" cried Yianoula. "Do you want everyone in the village to hear you?"

"So?"

She crossed herself in fear. "In the name of the Virgin, Christ does not rise until midnight."

Pavlo glanced toward the bedroom. "And how is the drama of birth proceeding?"

Yianoula silenced him. She grabbed the lit taper and blew it out.

"Why is everyone so quiet?" said Pavlo, seating himself beside Jason. His breath was heavy with wine. "In the name of Zeus, this is a good hour. God dies; a child is born!"

Yianoula asked him if he wanted some lentil soup but he slammed his hand on the table and shouted, "Friends of Livani, let me tell you about my wedding night . . ."

Yianoula threw him a menacing look.

". . . at my highest moment of ecstasy I heard strange noises outside our honeymoon cottage. I leaped out of bed and saw Yianoula's father, mother, sisters and brothers . . . the whole clan jammed against the front door, clamoring to get in. What else could I do? I put on the embroidered black velvet slippers which my new wife had presented to me earlier in the evening, and as soon as I unlatched the door they charged past me into the bedroom. I tell you, they were like savages, yelling and kicking, knocking things on the floor, throwing Yianoula off the bed. I became alarmed and said to her, 'Have I married into a family of lunatics? Why are they

8

making this terrible racket?' And this was her reply . . ."

"Pavlo!"

" 'They are looking for the stain on the sheet, my virgin stain'—ne, ti, ri, rem!"

Yianoula went into the bedroom but she did not stay long. After a battle of words, she was pushed back into the kitchen by the midwife. Pavlo slapped his thigh. "Friends of Greece, there is no cause for alarm. God the Father is not sleeping tonight, not while His Son is suffering."

Jason got up from the table. Seeking solitude, he strolled into the yard. An adolescent moon was crawling over the sky. He circled past the south grove and climbed the small hill to the chapel that his grandfather had built. He loved to come here as a boy. It was a refuge from his father's harsh voice, his mother's overbearing love, but looking at it now under the dim glaze of the moon, he saw how sadly neglected it had become. Most of the roof tiles were broken, the gold paint on the dome had chipped away, all four walls were cracked, chunks of stucco lay on the ground.

"Friend nephew, is that you?"

He concealed himself in silence.

"In the name of Zeus, I am speaking to you!"

"What do you want?"

"Are you John the Baptist? What are you doing out here in the wilderness?"

Jason started to move away.

"Are you worried about your mother? I tell you, this is a blessed night. We have nothing to fear."

"How did you know where to find me?" asked Jason.

"Water seeks its own level, friend Jason."

"What does that mean?"

"My eye has followed you from the day of your birth. You are exactly like my brother Stathis, a dreamer. How I rue that day when Uncle Philippos came to Livani with his fat cigar, his silk suit, pockets stuffed with American dollars! For

9

weeks he beleaguered us, boasting about his large restaurant in New York City, his two bank accounts, two cars. It was I who always yearned to go to America. I who should have been chosen. But no, Uncle Philippos placed his hand on Stathis' head and announced: 'I will make you a wealthy man in five years. One day my restaurant will be yours. Everything I have will be yours!' America did not want Stathis. She wanted me. But I am a patient man. My day will come soon. Friend Jason, I expect you to accompany me to America."

Jason laughed.

"Tell me about the Reserves. You were gone two whole years and this is the first chance I have had to talk with you. Did you like it?"

"Yes."

"Where did you train?"

"In Macedonia."

"What branch were you in?"

"Infantry."

"And how were the blond young maidens of Macedonia? I envy you—all that training and experience, but in the name of Zeus, I hope you are never called upon to use it."

Jason's thoughts flew to Kostaki. They were in the Reserves together. Kostaki had returned to Livani with him but stayed only a few days. After having seen Athens he fled from the village, vowing he would never come back.

It had been a different life in Athens, free and open, unfettered from provincial bonds and narrow minds. Jason had tried to explain all this to his father the first day back in Livani, and for the moment his father listened. Perhaps it was the uniform, the two years he had been away, but when his father saw that he meant every word he turned cold. A week passed. Two. The thought of being trapped in Livani for another summer terrified him, the arid days and windswept nights, the scorching suns, nowhere else to go but the taverna, no one to share his thoughts and feelings, chained like his father to two hundred olive trees. *Apostolic successors to the olive!*

And then one morning while walking across the square of Livani he saw Danae standing with her sick mother in front of her father's cobbler shop. The sun had cloaked her in a mantle of gold. But this was not the Danae of his childhood, pigtails and ribbons, timid, shy. In two short years Athena had transformed her into a goddess.

"Friend nephew, I am speaking to you!"

"What is it?"

"We have been here a long time. I think we should go back to the house."

The midwife was waiting for them on the porch, her shoulders heaving with sobs.

"What is going on here?" said Pavlo.

"May God forgive us," cried Yianoula from the kitchen. "It has happened again!"

Kyra Maria's eyes soared toward the ceiling. "I warned him, Holy Mother. A thousand times I warned him!"

Pavlo tried to enter the bedroom but the two women swarmed over him in a chorus of moans. Jason pushed them aside and looked into the bedroom. His father was not there.

"He grabbed the dead infant from Kyra Maria's hands and ran out of the house," exclaimed Yianoula. She looked faint.

"Where did he go?" asked Jason.

"I do not know."

The midwife slumped into a chair and started crossing herself. "This is an evil hour, an evil hour!"

A few moments later, Marko stomped into the kitchen, arms shaking, face ashen.

"What did you do with the baby?" Yianoula shrieked.

"I buried it."

"What?" screamed the midwife.

Yianoula was horrified. "How could you have done such a terrible thing without the priest?"

"I shit on the priest!" Marko bellowed. He washed his hands in the sink then slumped into a chair. All this time Pavlo did not say a word.

"Someone will have to attend to the afterbirth." The midwife frowned.

No one moved.

"You men are all alike, quick to take a woman's pleasure but not her pain."

Jason was assaulted by a repugnant odor when he entered the bedroom. His mother's eyes were open but she did not speak to him. Eons of pain seemed to cloud her face. He saw the white pan under the bed and quickly he reached for it. *Grandfather Andreas, you never spoke to me about this . . . blue-gray death swirling in blood and urine.*

His father hurled him a scornful look when he came into the kitchen with the pan. Pavlo kept his face turned. "Hurry, friend nephew. In the name of Zeus, the smell is eating me!"

After he reached the vineyard he put the pan down then went back for a shovel. He dug a hole and tilted the pan over it until everything slid into the ground with a soft plop. Fighting nausea, he filled the hole and ran back to the house. Yianoula took the pan away from him and washed it over the sink. After a long silence Pavlo rose to his feet. "And therefore, friends of Greece, life goes on."

"Where are you going?" Yianoula asked him.

"Into the bedroom."

"Why?"

"To offer some words of consolation to my sister."

"Not now. Katina is too weak."

"Then perhaps I should have a little lentil soup."

"How can you think of food at a time like this?"

"Because I am restless and uneasy. You know that I always get hungry when I am this way."

Despairingly she lifted her eyes toward the ceiling.

"Friend wife, do you expect to find God up there? *Our Father, who art in plaster, plastered be Thy name . . .*"

"Must you play the fool at a serious moment like this?" Yianoula exclaimed, wringing her hands.

The midwife opened the door to the porch. Her eyes were drawn, her shoulders sagged. "I must go to church for a while. When Katina feels up to it give her some warm milk."

Yianoula nodded.

Kyra Maria's heavy footsteps scraped over the porch floor. "I hope you have learned your lesson." Her voice sliced back at Marko. "Perhaps now you will keep that thing inside your pants!"

•　　　•

Jason awoke at daybreak and found his aunt adding wood to the jaki, preparing breakfast. His father had already left for the groves. Jason had a deep yearning to see Danae but there were too many things on his mind. Pavlo arrived at eight o'clock, carrying an earthen jug in his arms.

"Good, you brought the milk," said Yianoula.

"Friend wife, may I ask a theological question? Do you plan to give this milk to my sister?"

"Yes."

"On Holy Week?"

"The sick are not bound to the laws of fasting."

"Of course, I forgot," said Pavlo. He touched Jason on the arm. "Where is your father?"

"In the groves."

"In the name of Zeus, this is Holy Saturday. No one works today!"

Jason went into the yard to cut some wood and when he returned an hour later he found his father in the kitchen with Pavlo. Yianoula was heating some milk over the jaki. His father was unshaved, his hands soiled. Jason went to the window and stared at the morbid sky. *Holy Saturday*. In a few hours it would be all over, the fuss and turmoil, the hollow greetings, red eggs and roast lamb. *He is Risen! He is Risen!*

Yianoula brought the milk into the bedroom but came back

with a sour look. "Not one drop. She did not touch a single drop!"

Pavlo stirred. "The world is not lost, friend wife. Have you forgotten what happened after we pulled Renio out of your womb? For one whole week you refused to eat. Your face turned so frightfully yellow Charon the Ferryman began sharpening His teeth. I was so certain that you were going to die I summoned the priest but after chanting enough *Kyrie eleisons* to fill his Bible he too gave up in despair. And therefore, you kept melting away. Even my saintly grandmother could do nothing for you. Do you remember how she journeyed all the way down from Sparta, dragging her exorcisms behind her, then dabbing hot olive oil over her wrinkled forefinger and shoving it, begging your pardon, into your belly button, making three full turns around your prostrate body on the floor, mumbling her magic words? *A voice in the wilderness!* It was here that I decided to take matters into my own hands. I am not a religious man, mind you. In fact, I was always under the impression that God was only for old women and idiots, but something happened to me that night and I found myself running into the village and forcing the priest to open the door of the church. Wasting no time, I went immediately to the icon of Saint Chrysostomos and yelled into his face: 'Hey, Golden Mouth, must you sleep at a time like this? In the name of Zeus, my Yianoula is dying. Put on your robes and miter, call all the saints together and tell them what is happening here. Move!' Friends of Greece, Golden Mouth started crying before my very eyes, tears the size of diamonds. And therefore, when I returned home, there you were, friend wife, sitting at the table and gorging yourself like a starved goat. The fast was broken. But if I had not awakened Golden Mouth he would have kept snoring throughout the night and you would be in Charon's bowels today!"

Yianoula was not paying attention to him. She placed several dozen eggs into a large pot, filled it with water and put

14

it over the fire. Jason remembered how he always helped his mother with the eggs when he was a child. After they were dyed he would glaze them with a coat of olive oil and many times the eggs would slip out of his hands and fall to the floor but she never scolded him.

The midwife returned to the house in the early part of the afternoon, carrying a neatly wrapped bundle in her arms. Her son Fanoulis was with her: tall and gangly, eyes gawking, a silly smile frozen on his face. Jason felt a stab of pity, especially after Pavlo started in on him. "Friend Fanoulis, what are you doing here? You should be at your post. This is no time to abandon the church bell!"

With her busy hands, the midwife nudged her son toward the bedroom. "Go and pay your respects to Jason's mother. She is in there."

Fanoulis went as far as the door and peered inside, then, giggling, he ran out of the house. Kyra Maria seemed pleased. She put her bundle on the kitchen table and took off her black coat.

Pavlo sniffed loudly over the bundle. "What heavenly dish do we have here?"

"I baked some spinach pie for the Resurrection feast," said the midwife.

"Health to your hands, Kyra Maria," exclaimed Yianoula from the jaki.

Pavlo went to his wife and took her into his arms. "I think you should go home now, friend wife. Take a nap for a few hours. Kyra Maria is here. She will manage things."

Yianoula nodded.

Within moments the priest made his appearance. Bald and portly, a head shorter than Jason, he went first to Marko and said, "I heard the sad news from Kyra Maria. May God be merciful and heal your sorrow."

Pavlo jabbed his elbow into Jason's ribs. "It was the spinach pie that brought him here."

The priest cleared his throat. "Where is Mrs. Katina?"

"In the bedroom," said the midwife.

Pappa Sotiri gulped down the glass of wine that Jason offered him. "I have a brief respite before the evening service. I shall be quick about it."

"About what?" said Marko.

"I came to read over your wife."

"Not now. She is sleeping."

"It will only take a moment."

"You can come back another time."

"But it must be done now while the stain of Adam's sin is still upon her."

Pavlo slapped his thigh. "The truth is finally out. It was decrepit old Adam who stained Katina, not Marko!"

Everyone followed the priest into the bedroom. He placed his embroidered stole over Katina's sunken belly then lifted his hands. A hasty intonation, three *Kyrie eleisons*, the sign of the cross, and he was finished. After the others left the room Jason came beside the bed and spoke softly to his mother. "You must try to drink some warm milk."

She lowered her eyes.

"Kyra Maria brought us a spinach pie."

Her hand found his. It was cold and sweaty. He walked quickly to the window and closed it. Her eyes were red with tears when he backed out of the room. Pavlo and his father were sitting at the kitchen table. The priest was gone. Kyra Maria was washing something in the sink. Putting his hand over his heart, Pavlo rose to his feet. "Friends of Greece, what has happened to our noble heritage? Where is our glory? Plato and Aristotle have disowned us. Socrates holds his nose when we pass by. And why? Because we are more concerned with the belly than with wisdom."

"Where is the priest?" asked Jason.

"Pffft!"

The midwife had finished with the work at the sink and was about to take the eggs off the fire when suddenly she clamped both hands over her mouth. "In the name of the

16

Virgin, what happened to my spinach pie?" she cried.

"Ne, ti, ri, rem—ti, ri, rem. The goatbeard walked off with it."

Kyra Maria turned pale. "Why did you let him take it?"

Pavlo poured some wine into the glasses and sat down. *"Kyrie eleison, Kyrie eleison*—ne ti, ri, rem."

The midwife fled into the bedroom in a fit of sobs.

Pavlo glared at Jason. "How long must we shackle ourselves to this godforsaken village, to its primitive fears and superstitions? America cannot wait forever, friend Jason. In the name of freedom, if we remain in Livani we shall wallow in the dark ages. Look at us, a priest enters our house and we deem it necessary to show hospitality and give him a little something in return. 'For the Good,' as we say. Even from the days of Homer, hospitality has always been sacred to us. If you recall, this same hospitality proved to be the downfall of many Greeks, and particularly Menelaus, who opened all the doors of his home to Paris. But I am digressing . . ."

Jason felt restless. What was he doing here, listening to Pavlo's nonsense, confined in this narrow kitchen, playing the role of a dutiful son, hating every minute of it?

". . . there was a priest from my father's village of Psilopotamo who carried this custom to extremes. Everywhere he went he would say, 'A little olive oil, Christians, for the Good, for the Good!' Within a year he had gathered enough oil to fill a cistern which he secretly constructed in his cellar, a cistern five feet deep and gushing with rich Peloponnesian oil."

Kyra Maria came back into the kitchen, her eyes still wet with tears. She folded some cloths together and brought them into the bedroom. Pavlo waited until she closed the door. "That woman is a windmill. I often wonder how Orestes managed to hold her down long enough to produce even an idiot like Fanoulis. Bzzzt. Bzzzt. Have you ever seen two flies at it? But again I have strayed from our ill-fated priest. I say ill-fated because one day as he stepped into the cellar to admire his precious oil he slipped and plunged headlong into the cistern. His wife came rushing downstairs when she heard his frantic screams but what could she do? Fortunately several young men from the taverna also heard him and they dashed into the priest's house. When they saw the priest floundering in the oil, his face blue, his beard rolled up like a sausage, they shouted, 'Give us your hand, Pappa. Give us your hand!' But no, he refused. And so he drowned. And why? Because a priest does not understand the word *give*. He knows only *take, take!*"

The wine pitcher was empty. Jason's father, who was silent all this time, asked Jason to refill it. When Jason rebelled, Marko went downstairs himself, grumbling under his breath. Orestes joined them a few moments later. He did not speak, even after he downed his first glass of wine. Pavlo was furious. "Friend of the mandolin, can you not say something to the master of this house? In the name of Zeus, he has suffered a bereavement."

Orestes lifted his second glass to Marko and drank without saying a word.

Pavlo slapped his thigh in disgust. "At least tell us how the mandolin is these days."

"A mandolin is a mandolin."

"Are you trying to be a philosopher? Music and philosophy do not mix."

"What do you know about music?" Orestes laughed.

Pavlo jumped to his feet. "Do you want to hear a chant, a genuine Byzantine chant?"

"I would rather hear Jason sing," said Orestes.

"Of course. Hey, friend nephew, come away from that window. Why do you keep looking at the sky? Here, sit beside us and sing 'The Forty Guerrillas' the way your grandfather sang it!"

Jason stayed at the window. He remembered the exact moment when his grandfather branded him with a name he had never heard before. He was not yet five and they were

18

walking through the olive groves on a dry July day. '*My little Icarus, I have had my eye on you from the day you were born, those twitching little feet, those restless eyes. Someday you will put wings on your heart . . .*' That same night Jason heard him sing for the first time. The old man lifted him from the dinner table, held him in his arms, tickled his face with the point of his white mustache then, tossing back his proud head, he sang about the heroes of Independence: Diakos, Kolokotronis, Makriyiannis—their white steeds, their muskets, their scimitars coated with Turkish blood, their splendid ships cutting through the Aegean, the Attic sky quaking with their cries of freedom.

"Sing, friend nephew. Sing."

In the beginning, his voice was barely audible but as he moved into the heart of the song something seized him and he was once again that small boy nestled in an old man's arms. Everything became vibrantly real: the mustache tickling his face, the throbbing heart against his chest, the deathless voice:

> *Forty guerrillas from Livadia,*
> *Where are you going, lads,*
> *Where?*
> *To free Tripoli,*
> *Tripolitsa,*
> *From Turkish hands,*
> *And Ali Pasha!*

2

This was the only time of the year that Jason's father went to church. It was a long ritual that started late in the afternoon. He scrubbed his body clean with hard soap and water, shaved his face, trimmed his mustache, anointed his armpits and groin with rose water. Throughout the long ablutions he kept intoning the words, *'Behold the bridegroom cometh in the middle of the night!'* Despite her anguish and weak condition, Jason's mother smiled.

Yianoula prepared a light meal for them before it was time for church. Two suppers in one day, but she insisted, "The service will last for hours. If you do not eat, you will faint." Jason's mother tried to lift herself from the bed to join them but Yianoula prevented her, repeating over and over again, "All the chores are done. The house is ready for the Resurrection."

Little Renio sat with them in her pretty white dress and black shoes. Halfway through the meal she said to Jason, "You are not wearing your new suit."

"I am not going to church," he replied.

"Why not?"

"Because he has no need for God," Marko snapped.

Renio put down her spoon. "Come to church with us, Jason. Please come."

He tried to get away from the table but Pavlo held him down. "Friends of Greece, let us drink to that ill-fated creature, Christ. In the name of Zeus, here I stand like an English gentleman yet no one says a word. I am talking about this navy blue suit which I have named *Christ*. Yes, for one whole year it too lies buried, waiting to be dug out and resurrected."

No one laughed.

"Friend nephew, why do you do these things? Come now, get dressed. It is almost time for church."

"I said I am not going."

"But why not?"

"You are wasting your time," snorted Marko. "Ever since he came back from the Reserves he does not want to associate with us."

Pavlo kept at it. "You have a duty to your parents, to your uncle, to God!"

Marko slammed his fist on the table. "He is not listening to you. He is afraid we might adulterate his soul with our customs and beliefs."

"This is a serious matter," said Pavlo, putting down his glass of wine. "Jason was never like this. What changed him?"

"He thinks too much!"

"In the name of Zeus, he will be taken for a Communist."

There was a disquieting sound from the bedroom, the slow shuffle of bare feet over the floor. Body doubled over, both hands clutching her stomach, his mother struggled into the kitchen. Yianoula lost her patience. "Katina, get back to bed, this very minute!"

After everyone had quieted down, Yianoula cleared away the table. It was time for church. Pavlo waited until the others left the house before speaking to Jason. "Friend nephew, I see something in your eyes that convinces me you are unhappy here. Admit it. You delude yourself if you think you can solve all your problems by running off to Athens. Athens is still Greece, swarming with Greeks. You must make a clean break. There is no other way. Once we reach America you will appreciate what I am saying. Only then will you really be free!"

At last the house was silent. For a long while Jason sat at the kitchen table listening to his pounding heart, feeling his mother's disappointment. Torn with guilt, he hurried into his bedroom and put on his new brown suit. He tried to leave the house quietly, without her approval, but something drew him to her bedroom and he was rewarded by the rejuvenated smile on her face.

"Jason, come here by the bed," she whispered.

"What is it?"

"I want to talk to you."

"About what?"

"Your future."

He laughed.

"Please . . ."

He stepped inside but he did not go to the bed. Instead he stood by the window, staring into the darkness.

"Jason, why do you want to leave us?"

He did not answer.

"What are you seeking?"

My little Icarus, there is no greater joy in all the world than the wind dancing against your face, your heart soaring free of the earth's grasp . . .

"Jason, answer me."

After a long silence, he turned around and walked to the bed. Her hand reached out to him. When he took it, she closed her eyes and said, "I know what must be going on inside you. You are twenty-three. You have seen Athens. You have seen how the rest of the world lives. Probably you have slept with women."

"You do not understand," he said, moving away from the bed.

She called him back. "There are girls here in Livani, good girls from respectable families. You could marry one of them, have children, live here and be happy."

He moved away from her again.

"Jason, at least promise me this . . ."

"I cannot."

"Please say you will not leave until the end of summer."

"Why?"

"It is only a few more months," she said, gripping him with her eyes.

"We have gone over this a hundred times. I am leaving on the last day of June."

"Do it for me, Jason. Wait until September."

"It will not make any difference."

"Please?"

He almost ran out of the bedroom. When he stepped into the yard he breathed deeply several times until he grew calm. The olive leaves were being caressed by the wax fingers of the moon. A million stars adorned the night. Approaching the square, he saw a large crowd overflowing from the church and spilling into the street. He forced his way through the glowing faces and finally made it into the church. The smell of incense suffocated him. He pushed deeper into the standing throng and eventually he found a narrow space next to the chanter's stand. It lay just below the icon of God's eye. From inside the closed altar Pappa Sotiri's voice sounded cracked and tired.

> *Behold, we go up to Jerusalem,*
> *Where the Son of Man shall be betrayed*
> *Unto the high priests,*
> *And they shall condemn Him to death.*

There was a sudden commotion at Jason's elbow. Manolis the tavern-keeper was whispering into Yeros Panayiotis' ear. "Did you bring it?"

The old man cupped his hand over the ear.

"The musket, you old fool. Did you bring it?"

Yeros Panayiotis squeaked out a laugh then tapped the canvas bag he was carrying under the other arm.

"How about the blank cartridges?"

Again Yeros Panayiotis pointed to the bag. On the other side of Jason old Theologos had his musket perched on his bony shoulder in plain view of everyone. "Christ will not stay buried long tonight," he chirped, eyes flashing mischievously.

Barba Manolis drew courage and tugged free a shiny pistol from his coat pocket just as all the lights in the church went out. After a brief moment of silence Pappa Sotiri's high-pitched voice bounced against the dome.

Come, receive the Light,
And praise Christ,
Who has risen from the dead.

The heavy oak door of the altar swung open and the weary priest revealed himself to the congregation. He held two lit tapers in his hands and began swirling them high above his head, chanting, "Christ is Risen! Christ is Risen!"

At that same instant Barba Manolis pointed his pistol in the air and fired. Yeros Panayiotis was having trouble with his musket. It refused to shoot. Undaunted, Barba Manolis sent two more blasts of blank cartridges into the air.

"In God's name," shrieked the priest. "I command you to stop!"

As more shots resounded from Barba Manolis' pistol, someone outside the church began firing a musket. Within moments a volley of musket shots was heard from the street. The priest was white with rage. "This is a sin against Christ. You mock His Resurrection. If this does not stop immediately I will send you to your homes with the sin of an Unrisen Christ on your souls!"

But, even as he spoke, there was a devastating explosion outside. The holy lights in front of the icons dipped and swayed, the floor of the church rumbled. Someone had touched off the old cannon in the square!

Pappa Sotiri was at the brink of tears. His lit tapers hung weakly from his hands, their molten wax dripping over his vestments. "In God's name, I beseech you to stop!"

Jason had had enough. He pushed his way through the crowd and came into the vestry. He saw his father firing his old shotgun through the open door. Pavlo was at his side, elatedly pounding him on the back and encouraging him to fire again. Before Jason reached the street, the tumult subsided. The priest resumed the liturgy, passing through the open door and standing on the steps to announce that Christ was Risen.

Jason listened to the rest of the service from the street. After the Easter hymns were sung by the chanter, Pappa Sotiri brought out the gold chalice for the Eucharist. As a child Jason had always waited for this exalted moment:

You, who have fasted from the first hour, come and partake of this glorious feast. You also who have fasted from the sixth hour. And even you who have not fasted at all, for this is a holy and magnificent day, and everyone is invited to the table.

But now the words were meaningless and empty.

He caught sight of Danae on the other side of the street and he rushed to meet her. She was wearing a red coat and a white straw hat. "I did not think that you would be here," she murmured.

"Why are you not inside?" he asked.

"I could not get into the church. I have never seen such a large crowd."

"They come once a year," said Jason.

"Like you," she laughed.

The sound of her voice, her touch, her face . . .

"Did your mother give birth yet, Jason?"

"The child was born dead."

The genuine look of sorrow. "Was it a girl child?"

"No, a boy." Jason felt uncomfortable talking about it. "I hope you have not forgotten."

"What?" she asked.

"To meet me on the quay, after the Easter dinner."

"I will be there."

"Before the sun goes down?"

"Yes."

He clasped her hand.

People were filing out of the church, holding their lit tapers. The sky resounded from the echo of their greetings: "*Christ is Risen! Christ is Risen!*"

Jason bent down and picked up a small stone from the street, shifted it from one hand to the other, rubbed its rough surface with his fingers. *In the war, little Icarus, the great war against the Turks, I climbed to the summit of the Acropolis my first day in Athens. A heavy rain pelted down at me. I was alone. At my feet lay thousands of small stones. I picked one up and was about to toss it away when suddenly it spoke. "I am God. I have felt the warm feet of Socrates. Homer's blind lips kissed me!" I could not believe what I heard. I cupped it in my hands and waited for it to say more. I lost all thought of time and place, the war. I was aware only of that throbbing stone in my hands. In a wild moment, I said to myself, "Take it with you, this stone that calls itself God. It will comfort you in sorrow, heal you in sickness, resurrect you from death." And so, I put God into my pocket but as I walked away from the Acropolis a haunting feeling possessed me. In desperation, I reached into my pocket and withdrew the stone. Its brilliance so blinded me, so overwhelmed me with guilt and shame, I ran back and placed it on the exact spot from which I had taken it. Yes, my little Icarus, for one fleeting moment I had God in my hands . . .*

"Jason, what are you thinking?"

He released her hand. "The quay, just before sunset. I will be waiting for you."

He hurried to join his father who had just reached the gate of the schoolyard. Before Jason could say a word to him, he was manacled by Pavlo. "Friend nephew, are we Turks? In the name of Zeus, give me your hand and tell me that Christ is Risen."

"He is truly Risen," responded Jason.

"Now greet your father who is standing right beside you."

Jason turned and faced his father. "Christ is Risen."

"He is truly Risen," mumbled Marko. He had his mind on the lit taper and seemed anxious to bring it home before the wind blew it out. Nevertheless Jason detected a warmth in his eyes. The obedient son had complied with his wishes.

"You must not forget little Renio," Pavlo continued.

Jason picked up the child. She was thrilled to see him and hugged him with all her strength. "Christ is Risen," she exclaimed.

"He is truly, truly Risen." He smiled.

"Friend nephew, did you see your father fire the shotgun?"

"Yes."

"Why are you making a face? Christ is a sound sleeper. We have to produce all this noise to awaken Him."

Jason put Renio down but she held on to his hand. Pavlo shouted greetings to everyone in the square. When he saw the old men standing in front of the taverna, he began chanting:

> *Christ is Risen from the dead,*
> *Trampling death by His own death,*
> *Granting eternal life,*
> *Even to those in the tombs.*
> *Ne, ti, ri, rem!*

Jason glanced back, hoping to catch a last glimpse of Danae, but the crowd had engulfed her. His father had managed to protect the lit taper from the wind and as soon as they entered the house he went directly to the bedroom and lit the holy light on the icon shelf. His mother crossed herself three times. It was done. Their house would be safe for another year. No evil would befall them, no sickness or famine, no blighted olives. A mere flick of candle flame and the miracle was wrought.

The scent of roasting lamb drenched the house. Jason's mother insisted on joining them at the table. Yianoula brought out the red eggs for the cracking. Pavlo was the first to make a selection, measuring each egg, feeling and rolling it over in his hands. They cracked eggs with each other and in the end only Renio's egg remained unscathed. She was proclaimed the egg-cracking champion of the Peloponnesus by Jason.

In the groves a nightingale awoke and started singing to the resurrected sky. The stars had already fallen asleep. A few more breaths and the sun would be stretching his raw fingers over the world.

3

The winds of spring embraced Greece. It seemed she could not wait to fling away her winter veil of mourning, to burst into new beauty, to dance, to sing. Jason's mother was purified after forty days and although she tired easily she came with them to the festival of the Pentecost. Picnic tables lined the schoolyard. Orestes and his mandolin players were already seated on a platform under the shade of an ancient plane tree. The air was saturated with the aroma of food: whole lambs on the spit, sausages sputtering, chickens roasting, freshly baked bread, bowls of cheese, olives, fruit, and barrels of wine. Marko walked Katina to a vacant table. She wanted to help Yianoula with the tablecloth and plates but Yianoula would not allow it. The mandolin players broke out with a *Sirto* just before the food was passed around. Pavlo pushed himself away from the table and stood up. "Friends of the festival, we came here to dance!" Drawing out a handkerchief from his trouser pocket, he spun it around a few times then offered one end to Marko. Old Theologos spotted them and came limping forward. In time eight men joined the circle. Pavlo was obsessed. He twisted and turned, leaped high in the air and slapped both heels like a Cretan warrior. Old Theologos urged him on, shouting, "Opa! Opa!" Marko had all he could do to hold him up and prevent him from falling. Spurred by the loud roar of approval from the crowd, one of the women stepped forward and presented Pavlo with a glass of ouzo which he downed without missing one step. He flung the glass away and went into a series of dizzy spins, high leaps, and more loud slaps at the heel. When the dance finally ended, he came back to the table and reached for the bottle of wine but Yianoula took it away.

"Friend wife, there is no sin in a glass of wine. In the words of God, 'Wine maketh the heart of man to rejoice!' "

Pappa Sotiri was sitting at the next table and overheard him. "David spoke those words, not God."

"Who is David?"

"Eat," said Yianoula, pointing to his plate of food.

"I need a little wine to encourage my appetite."

She picked up a morsel of lamb and held it before his face. "Encourage it with this!"

He took a savage bite. Jason saw his mother pull out a handkerchief from her purse and with a shaking hand wipe her brow.

"Are you ill?" he asked.

"I feel fine," she said.

"You look pale," Yianoula exclaimed.

"There is nothing wrong with me. Please eat, all of you."

Marko stopped eating. "Something has upset you. What is it?"

"The priest . . ."

"What about him?"

"When he turned to speak to you, I remembered the vow . . ."

"What vow?"

"After I became pregnant again I got frightened. I did not want to lose the child."

"So?"

"I made a vow to the Virgin. I promised her that if she granted me another son I would dedicate him to the church."

Marko stood up. "You vowed to make my son a priest, a goatbeard?"

She nodded tearfully.

"I am glad he died!" Marko yelled, banging his fist on the table.

Pavlo was shaking his head in disbelief. "Friend sister, how could you have done such a thing without first consulting with your husband or with me?"

"It was Great Friday. I felt certain that the child was going to be born on that day."

"So what?"

"Not every child is born on Great Friday. I saw it as a divine omen."

Pavlo crossed himself with his left hand. "Friend sister, have you so quickly forgotten that little Renio opened her eyes to the world on the day John the Baptist was beheaded? Did this mean that we had to lop off her head also? You speak of omens. What about your Aunt Eudoxia? Poor unfortunate creature, she showed her face on the feast day of the Samaritan Woman, that same harlot who confronted Jesus at Jacob's Well. Even from a great distance, He knew what kind of woman she was. 'You have five husbands and you are not married to any of them!' And therefore, ill-fated Eudoxia chose that day to make her grand entrance into the world. The news spread into all the surrounding villages and before the sun went down hordes of people flocked around Eudoxia's house, wailing into her mother's face. 'Your daughter was born on an evil day. She will end up a whore with five men on her tail, just like that Samaritan Woman!' They worked Eudoxia's mother into such a state she was ready to toss her little baby over the nearest cliff in the custom of our Spartan ancestors, but thanks to your Great-uncle Cosmas, all those cackling people were driven out of the house and Eudoxia managed to live out her life with only one husband."

Jason had no further desire for food. He could not see Danae anywhere. Was her mother seriously ill? His father had become sullen, not speaking to anyone.

Pavlo had more to say. "Friend sister, you should have learned a lesson from me. Have you forgotten that our father, God forgive his soul, almost made me a priest? I was twenty at the time and at the peak of my manhood. But I was dissipating my life, refusing to work, gluing my ass to the taverna every day, smoking hashish, chasing skirts. After a few months of this, my cheeks turned pale and my clothes looked eight sizes too large. One night after I came home drunk and reeling from the hashish, our father filled my head with lumps. 'I am taking you to the seminary at Tripoli,' he exclaimed. 'You will make a fine priest. You hate work, you sleep all day, you always have your hand out!' From the look in his eyes I knew he meant every word. And therefore, I got up early the next morning and took the goats into the hills, staying with them for three whole days until I was certain our father had cooled his head. From that moment on, I never smoked hashish, nor did I chase another skirt. In the name of Zeus, I got married and that was the end of my dissipated life."

A smile crept over Katina's face. "A fine priest you would have made!"

"Begging your pardon, whatever priests can do I can do also: eat, drink, sleep, beget children, light candles, chant a *Kyrie eleison*—ne, ti, ri, rem." He stopped abruptly and turned to Jason. "Friend nephew, what do you say to all this? Wait, you need not answer. I know what goes on inside your brain. I am traveling that same road. Livani is a horrible prison, oozing with fears and superstitions. But this will all change. As soon as we reach America we will be liberated. Free! The moment we set eyes on the Statue of Liberty all our problems will be solved."

"Shut up," yelled Marko. "I am sick and tired of it, you and America. You know damn well that you will never go there!"

Pavlo did not get angry. He threw his arm over Marko's shoulders and said, "Friend of the olive, now that sufficient time has elapsed and your marriage to my sister has survived the cruel vicissitudes of life, I want her to tell you the truth."

"About what?"

"Tell him, Katina; tell him about Loukas."

Katina became uneasy.

"In the name of Zeus, tell him!"

"Pavlo, please be quiet," said Yianoula.

"Very well, I will tell him. It is about time he knew."

"Knew what?" said Marko, leaning forward on the table.

"Another man was in love with my sister before you stole her from under my father's nose."

"What man?"

"My second cousin, Loukas."

Marko let out a roar.

"Why are you laughing?" said Pavlo.

"Your second cousin was in love with Katina?"

"Yes. He wanted to marry her."

"That is ridiculous."

"I too was in love with him," said Katina softly.

"What?"

"He was kind and very gentle."

The veins of Marko's arms swelled. "Did he screw you?"

"Marko!" exclaimed Yianoula, glancing with horror at the nearby tables.

Marko glared at Katina. "You were in love with him and he was in love with you. Did he screw you?"

Pavlo grabbed him by the shoulders and hoisted him to his feet. "Friend of the olive, I will not permit you to talk like this to my sister. Do you hear? No one screwed her except you. But in the name of Zeus, there are times when I wish it had been Loukas."

"It is not too late," Marko ranted. "She can still go to him!"

Katina's voice trembled. "Loukas is dead. He died of malaria in Egypt." She started to weep.

Marko sat down again. "Does this mean that I have you all to myself now?"

Jason stood up.

"Where are you going?" Marko asked.

Jason looked at his mother before walking away. Her eyes were still wet. Yianoula's attention was on Renio, trying to get her to eat but the child wanted to go with Jason. Yianoula warned her to keep quiet.

The harbor was only a few hundred yards from the schoolyard. When Jason got there he took off his shoes and started walking barefoot along the water's edge. A large ship was plowing up the coast, unfurling a white ribbon of spray in the sea. A family of gulls circled gracefully above it, dipping and gliding with the wind. He was entranced by their flight.

"Jason!"

Danae's voice startled him. He looked back and saw her racing toward him along the shore. Her brown hair was being whipped back by her swift movement, her red skirt and white blouse hugged her body. She too was barefoot and held her brown leather sandals in her hand. He waited until she approached then swept her into his arms. Her face was the color of autumn grass. He kissed her then walked with her along the edge of the water. They turned at the high cliffs above the harbor and started climbing. At the top they found a sheltered nest of rocks and sat. Her nearness tormented him. From the day he returned to Livani he longed to be close to her, even for a few moments. It made no difference where, in the field of poppies that enclosed the ancient temple to Poseidon, here on these cliffs, beneath the tall cypresses at the entrance to the north pass, in the quiet cemetery at the crest of Livani's highest hill. They rarely spoke. He was content just to look at her, to touch her.

"Jason . . ."

33

"What is it?"

"I have to tell you something."

He reached for her hand.

"The reason I have not wanted you to make love to me . . ."

"Danae, you do not have to explain."

"But I do. It is because . . ." She turned her face away from him and looked down at the sea. "A voice deep inside wants you to make love to me but I block my heart so that I will not hear it."

"I do not understand," he said.

"If we get involved with each other you may never go to Athens." A tear trickled down her cheek and he leaned forward to brush it away.

"Danae, if only you knew how much I want you, how much I desperately want you."

Her eyes touched his.

"This damn village," he said, slamming his fist into his hand. "How I detest this goddamn village with its prowling eyes and filthy tongues!"

"Jason, you must not blame the village. It is our own fault. We never should have fallen in love with each other. You are free to leave Livani and you must do it."

"What about you?"

"I have no choice. I must stay here because of my mother."

"But what if you had a choice?"

She smiled. "I would go to Athens tomorrow."

"To Athens?"

"Jason, I do not want you to laugh. When you were away in the Reserves and I was in school in Sparta, I had a teacher who opened my heart to archeology."

"Archeology?"

"Why are you grinning?"

"I just never expected you to say something like that." He let go of her hand. "This teacher in Sparta, is he young?"

Danae laughed. "She is a woman. She has traveled every-

34

where—Italy, Egypt, Turkey, Africa. She plans to go to one of the islands this summer."

"For what?"

"To excavate. She is joining a group that hopes to locate the actual site of ancient Atlantis. I wish I could go with them."

"What is holding you back?"

"I told you. It is because of my mother. She does not want me out of her sight. She cries whenever I mention it." Danae looked down at the sea once again. "There are times when I suspect she is not really sick, that it is an act to keep me by her side. One day, before you came back from the Reserves, I made up my mind to leave but then I was torn with guilt."

"Why?"

"If anything had happened to her while I was gone, I would never have forgiven myself."

"What about your father?"

"He loves her . . ."

There was a sudden noise behind them, the sound of falling rocks. Jason spun around and saw the toothless smile of Fanoulis. He tried to wave him off but Fanoulis kept gawking at them. Jason decided to ignore him and in time Fanoulis disappeared behind the rocks.

"We should go back," sighed Danae.

He helped her down from the cliff and when they reached the shore she put on her sandals and walked ahead. He slipped into his shoes and kept a few paces behind, watching her legs, her swinging arms, her hair. He caught up to her just outside the schoolyard. "Will I see you tonight?"

She did not turn around. "Where?"

"At the north pass."

She nodded. He waited until she was lost in the lines of dancers that were snaking their way around the tables. Moving into the throng, he saw his mother talking to Pappa Sotiri.

Yianoula and Renio were putting away the food. Pavlo was lying on a blanket, snoring.

"Icarus!" snorted his father, looking up from the table in a drunken stupor.

4

Thirty-seven musicians. This was the name Livani gave to his grandfather's sheep. Each had its distinctive bell strapped under the neck. *Little Icarus, you must learn to listen carefully. There, can you hear that old nanny? She has the lowest sound of all.* Every afternoon as they passed through the square after a day in the hills they were met by the usual welcoming committee. *Here comes grandfather Andreas with his orchestra!* Jason felt proud walking at his side, drawn to that crop of white hair, the straight back, the noble countenance. Even the sheep seemed to respond, their little feet bouncing over the cobblestones, their bells singing—and when they passed the old men seated in front of the taverna, his grandfather greeted them with a twist of his mustache, a toss of the head. It was an icon forever engraved in Jason's mind.

"Athenian, we are waiting."

"Marko, there is no need for Jason to come," he heard his mother say.

"You keep out of this."

"But I am only going to see a doctor."

"I want him with us," said his father. "There are mares for sale in Kalamata. He has a good eye for animals."

The old mare was already hitched to the wagon. She finished eating the pail of oats and began swishing her tail when Marko gave her water. Jason waited until his mother and father were seated on the wagon then reluctantly he stepped around the back and climbed on. As soon as they reached the street Pavlo came out of nowhere and seized the reins, pulling the mare to a halt. "In the name of Zeus, did you think you could leave Livani without me?"

"This is not a pleasure trip," growled Marko.

Pavlo climbed on the wagon and sat between Marko and Katina. Glancing back, he remarked, "Ah, we have the soldier with us. Friend sister, what is the purpose of this journey?"

"Marko wants me to see a doctor in Kalamata."

"Why?"

"It is none of your business," yelled Marko.

"A doctor, you say? You are wasting your time and your money. Who of us has ever been cured by a doctor?"

Marko gave a fierce yank to the reins and the mare snorted forward. They took the sea road, which was downhill most of the way, but at Psilopotamo, where they came to the first hills, the mare slowed down to a walk. She dumped two huge loads in front of them, causing Pavlo to pinch his nose. "Friend mare, is this your only concern in life: into one hole and out the other? In the name of Zeus, you cannot live by oats alone."

"Shut up!" Marko exclaimed.

Pavlo took off his cap and crossed himself. "Friend of the olive, I had an uncle exactly like you. Theodoris was his name. You are ass-and-underwear with him—the same bad manners, sour disposition, vile curses. Uncle Theodoris could outcurse a Cephalonian."

"I sleep with your damn uncle!"

"There you go again. And therefore, Uncle Theodoris had a deep passion for cards. I can still see him in the taverna, that old leather cap tilted over his eye, clutching his cards with one hand while the other fidgeted with his nose, his mustache, his eyebrow. Like all gamblers, he was extremely high-strung. Friends and travelers, there is a lesson to be drawn from all this. One day he was at it again in the taverna when suddenly he flung his cards into the air and let loose a torrent of curses at the Virgin. 'Hey, Theodoris,' all the men yelled, 'show a little respect. Have you no shame, cursing the Holy Mother that way?' Uncle Theodoris laughed in their faces. 'Tell her to deal me better cards and I will show respect.' But unfortunately his cards did not improve and Uncle Theodoris filled the taverna with curses once more. Just then the old priest walked in. He grabbed Uncle Theodoris by the ear and hoisted him to his feet. 'Repent,' he cried. 'Repent for your sinful blasphemies against the Holy Mother or I will personally condemn you to everlasting hell!' The next day at cards he kept drawing bad hands but did he curse the Virgin? No. Instead, he took off his old leather cap and spat into it. 'In the name of the Father,' everyone remarked, 'Theodoris has finally mended his ways. Look, no longer is he cursing the Virgin. He is taking out his wrath on that dirty old hat.' And thus it went for many years. When Uncle Theodoris finally closed his eyes for the last time, he left only one request, that he should be buried with his leather cap on. At first, the priest agreed but that dirty old hat bothered him so much he reached into the casket in the middle of the service and yanked it off Uncle Theodoris' cold head. Sewn inside it was a miniature icon of the Virgin. Her face was so distorted and caked with spit, it did not look like the Virgin at all . . ."

He was still jabbering away when they entered Kalamata. It was midday. The streets were crowded. Workers were leaning out of the open windows of the flour factories, their bleached faces gasping for air, speechless, like figures in a puppet theater. *Manikins*. Painted faces over painted dreams, everyone a manikin: Pavlo the court jester of the Peloponnesus, his father the scarecrow of the olive groves, Danae tied to her mother's bed while dreaming of ancient Atlantis, and he wanting desperately to adorn himself with wings!

He felt strange, sitting alone in the back of the wagon. His mother turned around to glance at him and immediately he recalled how he had always loved to hear her speak about her ancestry . . . a captivating story of Italian princes, of ships and treasures, beauty and love. Over his father's stinging barbs, she would whisper into Jason's ear, narrating each event, lifting her voice at the most climactic moments: an unfolding drama of two young men from Florence, sons of the Medicis, who had violated a rich Italian girl and had to escape from their country, stowing away on a brigantine, then, as it approached the southernmost tip of the Peloponnesus, jumping into the sea and swimming two miles to the very edge of Taenarus where they were found sprawled on the rocks half-dead. The people of Livani took them into their hearts and nursed them until they were well and strong. They taught them Greek letters and customs and after a few years they married the two most beautiful girls of the village, and from this lineage came Jason's mother, a daughter of noble birth.

At another time, when he was still that age, he would beg his father to tell him about his courtship, how his father rebelled at the thought of a matchmaker handling all the arrangements, how he himself led Katina's father into their spotless parlor and told him he wanted to marry his daughter.

'What dowry do you demand?' asked the father.
'Dowry? I just want your daughter.'
'I am sorry, but I cannot agree to the marriage. You are too young and unworldly. You need seasoning, my boy. Salt. Lots of salt!'

And the very next morning his father hurried back to Katina's house, driving four mules and an eight-wheel wagon filled with salt. When Katina's father saw this, he roared with laughter and warmly gave his blessing.

But now Jason felt a bitterness in his heart. He could not

understand why things had to change, why people grew old and love had to die.

The wagon proceeded across a busy square and pulled into a wide street where two old women, elegantly dressed, stopped to gaze at them. After another half-mile, his father gave a hard pull on the reins and the mare came to a halt before a large white house of stucco. On the black front door, painted in bold white letters, was the name: NIKOLAOS ANDRAKOS, DOCTOR OF MEDICINE.

•　　•

A well-dressed man, dignified and with a mild voice, answered the door. He escorted them into a small waiting room and motioned toward a lumpy brown couch. Two matching chairs were pushed back against one wall. Above the chairs, an ancient clock ticked loudly, breaking the silence. On a small marble-top table rested a slender blue vase filled with fresh flowers. An open door led to an inner office. It was spotless—a glass cabinet with symmetrical rows of bottles, a smaller glass cabinet with shiny silver instruments, several shelves of books.

"Who is the patient?" he asked.

"My wife," said Marko.

"What seems to be the problem?"

"The midwife from our village has warned me never to touch her again."

"For what reason?"

"She has lost many babies."

The doctor gave Katina a sympathetic look. "I will give her a thorough examination but it may take some time."

"We are in no hurry," Marko gruffly replied.

Katina followed the doctor into the inner office. After a few moments another patient entered the waiting room, an emaciated old man with a sallow face. He was hunched over and had a difficult time seating himself in one of the chairs.

"More of God's mistakes!" snarled Pavlo with disgust.

The old man stared at the floor, lips moving.

"Friend Barba, you are waging a losing battle. It is too late to save those wretched bones!"

The man kept his eyes on the floor. Suddenly he broke into a grin.

"Laugh, Barba. Life is a comedy. What do you hope to gain from a well-groomed man of wealth who calls himself a doctor? If you had an ounce of sense you would pick up your bed and clear out of here."

"He cannot hear you," said Jason. "He is deaf."

"He speaks. My nephew speaks."

In the very next instant the old man's eyes became frozen once more. Pavlo stood up and started pacing around the waiting room. "Friends of Greece, beware of doctors and priests. One pecks away at your body, the other at your soul. When they get through with you, nothing is left, even for the worms. There is only one remedy for health and longevity: you must do exactly those things which doctors and goatbeards forbid. If you have never touched wine, never lied, stolen, cheated, looked upon a woman with lust, if you have relied upon pills and poultices, mustard plasters, manipulations and operations, I say unto you, 'Unbutton yourselves. Freedom is the only cure. Freedom!'"

It was five o'clock when his mother finally came out of the inner office. The doctor went immediately to Marko. "I am afraid the midwife's diagnosis was correct. Another pregnancy could prove fatal. Your wife's womb is abnormally twisted and . . ."

"How much do I owe you?" Marko barked. His hands were trembling.

"Ninety drachmas."

They followed the doctor through the narrow hallway. At the door, he stopped, and in a soothing voice, said to Marko, "It is not the end of the world. This does not mean you have

41

to stay away from her. You simply must take precautions. She understands. I have explained everything to her."

•   •

The mare had dropped another load in the street and flies were swarming over it. Marko tugged at the reins before Pavlo had time to seat himself, almost throwing him off the wagon. Dusk was invading the city. The manikins were no longer at the windows of the flour factories. The shops on Aristomenous Street were thronged with people.

"Friends of the Medical Society, shops stifle me. Living tombs! I knew a man who owned a tailor shop in Sparta . . ."

"Shut your mouth," yelled Marko.

They crossed the south bridge and skirted around the gulf. Half a dozen squalid huts loomed before them, roofs made of straw, scrawny goats scratching at the barren ground, children gazing at the wagon and waving, their parents guardedly watching from narrow windows and doors.

"In the name of Zeus, this is a cursed land, a rock pile! I cannot wait to get to America with my nephew Jason."

"I told you to shut your mouth."

"I am talking to myself."

"Grow up. Stop acting the fool."

"Grow up, he says! And become what, a toothless old man sucking at life one breath at a time?"

Fanoulis was the first person they saw when they entered Livani. He was scuttling across the dimly lit square on his way to the bell tower.

"Hey, friend Fanoulis, why are you going to church? Is this your wedding day? Wait for me. I want to sing Isaiah's chant for you and your bride. Ne, ti, ri, rem."

It came as a jolt to Jason: *they had not gone to look for a mare.* After all this time his father had never mentioned it again. He had never intended to buy another mare. But why did he insist that Jason come along? A man of iron on the outside but melted wax under the skin!

The bell sounded just as they pulled into the yard. His mother crossed herself three times. Jason unhitched the mare, led her into the barn, then rubbed her dry with a coarse towel. He gave her a bag of oats and when she finished eating he held a pan of water under her mouth. Perhaps Pavlo was right after all. Eating and drinking, life was no more than this. But it would be different in a few hours. He would be with Danae on the cliffs above the harbor.

5

He left for the mountains early the next morning, his thoughts still on Danae, reliving every moment they spent together—how they walked all the way from the harbor to the north pass, whispering each into the other's ear, then returning to the deserted square, sitting on the bench beneath the marble statue of Kolokotronis, listening to the swift flight of the wind.

But now he was alone, climbing the massive heights of Taygetus, not knowing where he was going, seeking the tallest peak. At noon he stopped under the porous shade of a wild olive tree and unstrapped his haversack. He ate half a loaf of bread and a large chunk of white cheese. After resting a while, he sliced his way through a mile-high gorge whose sides sparkled with brilliant veins of water. He stopped and drank from a small stream at the base of a cliff. An aura of peace clung to the air. Great birds drifted lazily in the sky. The song of cicadas wafted through the moist wind.

In the middle of the afternoon, he reached a jagged path that brought him up a sharp incline to the dizzy heights of a bald peak. Far below him, Livani looked like a dash of salt on the ground. To his left, where the earth touched the sky, he could see the dim lines of Kalamata converging into the Aegean. He pulled out the rest of the bread and cheese and sat down. The wind was bending the grass, sending tiny seeds into the air. Instantly his mind flitted to an unforgettable moment: *Saint Basil's Day*. The singing of the carols, the early morning breakfast, the noisy arrival of Pavlo and his family, the exaltation when the presents were opened in the front room. He remembered how his father came stomping into the house, dressed in a long-flowing robe, a false beard stuck to his face, pen and paper in hand. "Saint Basil! Saint Basil!" They all clapped their hands then sat at his feet to hear the prophecies, the threats and promises. After Pavlo and the others went home, his father dragged a burlap sack into Jason's bedroom and told him to open it. It was filled with barley seeds. Jason was heartbroken when he saw all those seeds but his father's eyes kept urging him to dig deeper into the bag until suddenly his hand touched a coin. With frantic fingers he plunged into the seeds and shouted with joy when he discovered another coin, still another. In time his father helped him. They spilled the entire bag on the floor and together they searched for the coins. Jason could not believe it. When they finally finished, hundreds of silver coins lay at his feet, the treasury of Midas. That night he was unable to sleep, but not because of the coins. For the first time in his life he had felt the warmth of his father's love:

> *Saint Basil is coming,*
> *With pen in his hand,*
> *Deep from Caesarea,*
> *The bountiful land.*

He was jolted out of his thoughts by the sound of bells. An old goatherd, lean and white-haired, stepped out of the rocks. Several dozen goats, covered with burrs, trailed behind him. They spotted a small patch of grass near Jason and fell upon it with loud bleats. Jason stood up to greet him then offered him the last of the bread and cheese.

"Whose son are you?" the goatherd asked.

"Marko Leonakos."

"Marko is your father?"

"Yes."

"Then Barba Andreas was your grandfather?"

"Yes," said Jason.

"I knew him well. We spent many nights together in the taverna. He was a great man, he and his thirty-five musicians."

"Thirty-seven," said Jason.

The goatherd almost choked on the bread. "The world is not lost over a few sheep. Do you by chance have a little wine in that haversack?"

Jason shook his head.

One of the goats tried to break away from the rest of the herd and started scrambling for the high ledge but the old man saw her. He cupped both hands over his mouth and yelled, "Frosso, get back here. Get back, you old witch!"

The nanny kept climbing. He picked up a stone and hurled it but it fell short. "Frosso, I will eat your liver. Come back. Do you hear me?" He spat out some of the bread in his mouth, shook his vein-streaked fist, and then in desperation turned to Jason. "Can you whistle?" he rasped.

"Yes."

"Then whistle, damn you. Can you not see that my mouth is filled? Whistle. Get that obstinate bitch back here!"

Jason put his fingers into his mouth and blew. Immediately the nanny stopped. He whistled once more and this time she came scrambling down from the ledge and joined the others. The goatherd was still seething. He picked up another stone and threw it but again it missed its mark. In time he calmed himself. After finishing with the bread and cheese, he dug his

45

hand into his trouser pocket and drew out a crumpled cigarette. "My name is Themistocles."

"And mine is Jason."

The goats now moved under a dwarfed olive tree and began attacking the leaves on the low branches.

"You are a long way from your village." Themistocles squinted.

"I love to climb," said Jason.

The goatherd took him by the arm. "Come, I want to show you something."

"What about the goats?" said Jason.

"I will keep an eye on them."

He led Jason into a deep corridor of rocks and then up that same ledge the nanny had tried to scale. From the top of the ledge, Themistocles pointed toward a distant peak. "There, can you see it?"

Through the thin clouds Jason made out a gray outline of stone jabbing the sky.

"That is the Monastery of the Living Blood," said Themistocles. "Now follow that precipice down . . . down. Do you see those half-dozen white houses? That is my village. It is called Akra."

"I never knew there was a monastery up there," said Jason.

"That precipice is three thousand feet high . . ."

Jason was spellbound.

"Your father never told you there was a monastery at Akra?"

"No."

"How many years do you have?"

"I am twenty-three."

Themistocles leaned back against a rock. Every so often his eyes flitted toward the goats who were still munching on the olive leaves. After a long silence he started telling Jason about the great war, his adventures in Smyrna and Turkey. Jason half-listened.

"You keep staring at that monastery like a bull drooling over a cow," exclaimed Themistocles.

"I find it very hard to believe," said Jason.

"What?"

"How anyone could have climbed that precipice, let alone built a monastery up there."

"Madness. Holy madness. I can tell you anything you want to know about those monks. I have had them in my hair since I was a child. Pious hypocrites! What good do they accomplish, running away from the world, hiding in their cells, singing *Kyrie eleisons* night and day?"

Slowly they came down from the ledge. Jason picked up his haversack and slung it over his shoulder. Themistocles whistled the goats together. "Tell me, what do you intend to do with your life?" he asked.

Jason's mind soared to the gray stones in the sky. *I want to fly over that mountain. I want to look down at the world from the highest throne of the universe.*

"Were you in the army?" Themistocles asked.

"Yes."

"Did you kill anyone?"

Jason laughed. "There was no war. I am in the Reserves. We were on maneuvers in Macedonia."

Themistocles let out another piercing whistle then turned sharply around. "Take my advice: pick up a hoe or a shovel. Work with your hands. Forget the head!"

"What makes you say this?" Jason asked.

"You have that look in your eyes, the look of a dreamer."

"Have you been a goatherd long?"

"Now and forever, amen!"

"Was your father a goatherd also?"

"You ask too many questions. You must drive your father insane."

"My father rarely talks to me."

"Can you blame him?" Themistocles snorted. Jason remained close to his side while he assembled the goats and nudged them down a narrow ravine. After a hundred yards the goats found another olive tree and made a frantic rush toward it but Themistocles stopped them, striking several in the rump with his knobby crook. They followed the ravine until they came upon a small field of grass. The goats dove into it with bouncing feet and this time Themistocles permitted them to eat. "Let me tell you something about that monastery," he said with a loud sigh. "You can credit the Turk. For four hundred years he pillaged this land, raping, burning, killing. But when his bloodthirsty feet tried to climb Taygetus, we cut them off. Yes, we kept harassing him and wearing him down until he finally gathered up his hashish and fled from these shores forever. During that time there was a saintly man living here whose name was Anagnostis. He was the only person in the entire county who knew how to read and write. One day he summoned everyone together and told them the Virgin had instructed him to build her a monastery as a tribute for driving the Turk out of Akra. He asked all his people to pick up shovels and ropes, spit into their hands, and follow him to the designated place but when they saw that awesome precipice stretching into the sky they dropped everything and ran back to their homes. Anagnostis pleaded with them and assured them there was no cause for alarm because the Virgin would guide each step they took. Well, Afenti Jason, three young men from a neighboring village volunteered to make the first assault on that precipice. They climbed almost one hundred yards, slipped and fell to their deaths, and again everyone fled to his home. But Anagnostis was persistent and begged them to return to the precipice. 'We will build a monastery to the Virgin,' they retorted, 'but not on that murderous mountain!' Over the learned one's protests, they selected another site and the work was begun. That night however the Virgin picked up their shovels and ropes and carried them to the foot of the precipice. 'You see,' exclaimed Anagnostis the next morning, 'the Virgin

48

wants her monastery built here, and here it must be!' With fervent determination, he slung a long rope over his shoulder and started climbing: one hundred feet, five hundred . . . up they went, Anagnostis and the Virgin . . . three thousand feet to the top of the mountain. After that, the rest was easy. He pulled up the others and in time the monastery was built."

Themistocles whistled to the goats and they moved on, down through another ravine, and into a wide plateau that was speckled with scrub pines and fragrant herbs. Jason's mind was still on the monastery. He tried to imagine what it was like inside: black-hooded monks strolling peacefully in a courtyard, candles flickering in a Byzantine chapel, voices chanting.

They followed the goats into a narrow gorge and came upon a wild stream that raced through a nest of fallen rocks. They stopped and drank. The water was ice cold. "I turn off here, Afenti Jason," said Themistocles.

"Perhaps we will meet again."

Themistocles signaled the goats to move on. "I am glued to these rocks. I have no wife, no children; nothing to my name but these mangy goats. It is not easy to live alone, especially after old age has turned you inside out. Go to the Good, Afenti Jason. Go with my blessing: may you never know how painful it is to shiver through life in a cold bed!"

He was gone, he and the goats absorbed by rock and wind. Within moments, the once-vibrant colors of the threshing floors were lost in purple shadows. Earth and sky became one.

6

It was Sunday again. Late in the afternoon, he went to the taverna to read the Athenian newspapers. Before sitting at a table near the window, he glanced across the square and saw the young girls strolling down the street, accompanied by their mothers. The same ritual, Sunday after Sunday. Yeros Panayiotis entered the taverna and hobbled directly to his table. Jason enjoyed reading the newspaper for the old man. His eyesight had failed but he had a curious hunger for news. Every page was crammed with the threat of war. Germany had already conquered Poland, Denmark, Norway, the low countries of Holland, Belgium, Luxembourg, and now they were converging upon France. Pavlo and a few others came drifting to the table when Jason started to read.

"In a matter of days, German mechanized divisions have poured into northern France from the Netherlands, capturing Abbeville, Boulogne, and Dunkirk. More than a quarter of a million troops were rescued by the British and French from the beaches of Dunkirk—but thirty thousand men died and almost all their equipment had to be abandoned. Hitler's rule over these conquered countries is barbarous. It is a government by terror, thousands being killed every day as hostages in reprisal for guerrilla attacks on German soldiers. Moreover, each of these conquered nations has been forced to enact legislation against all Jews, sending them off to Nazi concentration camps."

"What about the Italians?" asked Pavlo.

"They too have declared war on France. Their forces are invading southern France right now. Hitler and Mussolini are allies," said Jason.

"What has all this to do with Greece?" Yeros Panayiotis queried.

Barba Manolis tapped the old man on the shoulder. "Stop interrupting. We want Jason to continue."

Pavlo agreed. "Bravo, friend of the tavern. It is about time you acknowledged my nephew's military background."

Jason squirmed with uneasiness.

"Get on with it," cried Barba Manolis. "Tell us about

Greece. How does she plan to meet this threat from Mussolini?"

"Prime Minister Metaxas has quietly and methodically bolstered our country's defenses, and although he does not want to take any provocative steps, he is ready to strike back if the Italians make any move against Greece."

Yeros Panayiotis slammed his cane against the table. "My children, I predict that Greece will be in this war within a few months!"

"How can you predict anything?" Pavlo snickered. "You cannot see beyond your nose."

"Everything seems to be pointing toward war," said Jason.

Orestes, who had been sitting on the other side of Jason, stood up and began singing the anthem. Pavlo stopped him. "In the name of Zeus, what has happened to us? There are more important things in life than Hitler and Mussolini. I am sick and tired of listening to this nonsense, Sunday after Sunday. You all sound as if the world is coming to an end. For your information, we will still be here long after Hitler and Mussolini are blown away by the wind!"

"We cannot close our eyes to these grave matters," warned Master Theophilos. "Nothing is solved by burying our heads in the sand."

Orestes challenged Pavlo. "What is more important than the fate of your country? Do you want Hitler to do the same thing to us as he has to the Jews?"

"I want us to think about other things," exclaimed Pavlo. "Like what?"

"Like philosophy," said Pavlo. "Look at yourselves. The ancients would disown you if they could see your deplorable state. Your brains have deteriorated to such an appalling depth you do not even know what the word philosophy means."

Old Theologos hobbled into the taverna on his cane. "What have we here, a symposium?" he snickered.

"Sit down, grandfather. Sit down and enrich your mind

before Charon knocks at your skull. It is not too late. You still have time to fill that crusty old head with wisdom."

"We are waiting to hear your definition of philosophy," snapped Barba Manolis, moving from table to table, his apron slung over his shoulder.

"Friend of the tavern, philosophy deals with the problems of life. Any fool knows this."

"What about death?" asked Yeros Panayiotis.

"Death also, grandfather."

"Pavlo, the philosopher!" cried out Orestes.

Pavlo silenced him. "I know what all of you are thinking: 'That farmer, what does he know about life or death? His hands are caked with goatshit!' Friends of the Academy, I work by day but at night I fill my head with wisdom. And therefore, I am a true philosopher!"

Barba Manolis blew his nose and there was a small wave of laughter. Walking defiantly around the tables, both arms flailing, Pavlo yelled, "Answer me this, what training do all of you have for that eternal school of heaven? Panos, you cannot repair shoes up there. In the name of Zeus, there will be no coffee-brewing, no wine-making, olive-picking, card-playing, eating or shitting in that eternal school of heaven. But, unlike all of you, I have been preparing myself for that unavoidable day. I refuse to sit on my hands and wait for Charon to transport me across the Styx. I have a closet filled with books. I read. I think."

"Get on with it," said Barba Manolis. "Enlighten us about death."

"Slowly," cautioned Pavlo. "We are not brewing coffee here. Philosophy demands much time and patience."

Orestes turned to Jason. "Perhaps your nephew can tell us about death. He is a soldier; he should know."

"I cannot tell you anything about death," said Jason.

"Then speak to us of life."

My little Icarus, life is a child's initial carved on the trunk of an olive tree . . .

Pavlo came back to the table and slapped Jason on the back. "At last we are true Greeks. I am Plato and you, friend nephew, are Aristotle. In a short while our tavern-keeper will brew us a cup of nectar while the father of Fanoulis plays a tune on his lyre. In the name of Zeus, we have finally cast away all this drabble about Hitler and Mussolini and we are walking in the footsteps of our glorious ancestors!"

Yeros Panayiotis lifted himself up from the table and brandished his cane at everyone. "*I* will tell you what life is!"

"Speak, friend Socrates."

"When I was a young lad our favorite sport was to unbutton our trousers and see who could out-piss the other." He slammed his cane on the table. "I was a fountain. No one in Livani could match my stream!"

"But now," chuckled Barba Manolis, "that fountain cannot flow beyond your withered old toes."

"If it can get past his trousers first," laughed Orestes.

Yeros Panayiotis glared at the ceiling. "Blame Him, not me. Now I have told you what life is!"

"Drip, drip, drip," cackled Pavlo. After the laughter subsided, he added, "My lecture has come to an end. It is time to go our separate ways—you into darkness, I into light."

Jason pushed back his chair. It was almost dusk but the young girls were still walking through the square with their mothers, their neat and unruffled dresses clinging to their slender bodies, their eyes straight ahead, never glancing to the side.

Pavlo slapped his thigh in disgust. "Friend nephew, look at that ridiculous sight: the young virgins parading every Sunday, displaying their wares, trying to land themselves a husband. In the name of Zeus, we are living in the dark ages. On my mother's grave, I swear that I cannot endure this much longer. Friend Jason, the time has come for us to unbutton ourselves from this godforsaken place!"

Barba Manolis overheard him. "And go where?" he sneered.

"America, where else? Stop laughing, coffee-grinder. Do

53

you think I want to spend the rest of my life inside this taverna with you and those croaking old frogs? I know what you are thinking, but I was a young lad then, only sixteen. 'In America,' everyone was saying, 'gold flows in the streets!' And, therefore, I decided to make my move. I packed all my belongings, boarded the train at Kalamata and set off for Piraeus. Halfway up the gangplank I heard familiar voices: father, mother, sisters and brothers. Without breathing a word, they had come all the way from the village to see me off. Such weeping and gnashing of teeth! But like all Greeks they quickly brushed the tears from their eyes and began pushing me up the gangplank. 'In the name of Zeus,' I said to myself, 'am I a leper? Why are they so anxious to get rid of me?' And . . . therefore, friend of the taverna, I jumped off that gangplank and returned to the village. But I say it to you again, I was very young . . ." He stopped to wipe his eyes with the back of his hand. "If only I had climbed into that ship, I would be in America today . . ."

The bell for vespers sounded.

Jason looked up at the bell tower and saw Fanoulis pulling at the rope. Faithful Fanoulis. He held time in his hands. He told everyone in Livani when to sit, when to stand, when to work, when to sleep. They could not live without him yet everyone took him for an idiot.

TWO

Jason had never known such a summer. An inferno that scorched the earth, wilted the olive leaves, bleached the shoulders of Taygetus, dried up the cisterns and wells. A whole month passed without relief but his father refused to throw up his hands. While everyone else in the village knelt before the icon of Saint Chrysostomos, Marko worked, and although he never asked for Jason's help, the guilt was too much for Jason to bear. Together, they snipped off diseased branches, softened the earth around the trees, burned all the insect webs. One morning Jason smiled when he recalled a tale his grandfather loved to narrate about a fisherman who, after falling overboard in a storm, started to drown and in his great fear beseeched Saint Nikolaos to save him. "I will save you," replied the saint, "but first you must move your own arms."

The sun was about to explode when Yianoula appeared at the kitchen door on the hottest day of the drought. Renio was with her. Katina was happy to see them. A moment earlier, Jason and his father had just come in from the south grove. There was still much to do but the heat had exhausted them. Katina asked everyone to follow her into the front room where the shades were drawn. Marko chided Yianoula for exposing Renio to the sun.

"I begged her not to come," Yianoula retorted, "but no, she insisted on seeing Jason."

Jason took the child's hand and led her to the sofa. "Your face is pale," he said. He went into the kitchen and brought back a glass of water. Turning away from Renio, he poured a little ouzo into the glass then gave it to her. "Here, drink this. It will make you feel better."

She pushed the glass away. "I am not sick, Jason. Why should I drink it?"

"I want to see the color return to your cheeks."

"It has an awful smell."

"It is only water," he said.

"I saw you pour the ouzo into it. See, it is turning white."

Smiling, he held the glass against her lips until she took a sip. "There, that was not so difficult," he said, patting her on the head.

"Are my cheeks red, Jason?"

"Not yet. You must finish the rest."

She pecked once more at the glass, gasping after each sip. "Have they turned red now, Jason? Have they?"

"Yes, they are glowing with health."

She ran to the chair to show her mother and then came dashing back into his arms. "Three of our sheep died yesterday, Jason."

"I know."

"Their bellies swelled and their tongues hung out."

He poured himself a glass of ouzo. His father was not drinking.

"Jason, why did they have to die?"

"Hush!" cried Yianoula. "It was God's will."

"But why should God want them to die?"

Yianoula crossed herself. "I asked you to be quiet!"

"Answer the child's question," said Marko.

Yianoula gave him a menacing look. "The paths of God are unfathomable. We must believe and never ask questions."

"Goatshit. Where is Pavlo?"

"Home," said Yianoula dryly.

"Are you sure he has not gone to church to pray with the others?"

She crossed herself again. "If God does not help us who will?"

"They have been at it for a month," Marko scowled. "I should think God would have heard them by this time."

"Marko, I do not like to hear you talk like this," interjected Katina.

Marko leaned over and playfully pinched her on the cheek. Despite the heat and drought, he was relaxed and in good spirits. Glancing toward Renio, he said, "How do you feel, my little flower?"

She blushed.

"We must put more flesh on you. In a few years we shall be marrying you off to the richest man in the Peloponnesus."

"I am not getting married, Uncle Marko."

"Why not?"

"Because I want to sing the miroloy at funerals."

"Silence!" exclaimed Yianoula.

"What is wrong with that?" said Marko. "My grandmother sang the miroloy. She was such a tiny thing, so fragile and delicate, but she had the most beautiful voice in Laconia. People came from great distances to hear her. I was five years old when I listened to her for the first time. It was at a neighbor's house and as I stood next to the corpse . . ."

"Have you no shame, filling a child's head with such terrifying things?" Yianoula wailed.

"Marko, please stop," Katina begged him.

He paid no heed to them. "When my grandmother was eighteen she went on a pilgrimage to Jerusalem and was baptized in the River Jordan by a priest from the Church of the Nativity. She stayed many months in Jerusalem and eventually became a healer. Soon after her return to Kyparissia every sick person in the county came to her for help. Hundreds of healings were recorded and after she died they called her The Saint of Kyparissia."

"It is a pity you did not take after her," frowned Yianoula.

Marko smiled. "There was a small dark room in her house, just off the kitchen, where she consulted with the sick. I used to peek inside the door and watch her manipulate her hands over their heads and bodies. But, for me, her greatest gift was the miroloy." He stopped to glance once more at Renio. "Do you really want to learn the miroloy, my little flower?"

"I do," she said, jumping to her feet with joy. "I want to be exactly like your grandmother, Uncle Marko!"

His eyes watered. "Then you must begin as soon as possible. Attend every wake, every funeral. Study the words, listen while others sing, hear how forcefully yet soothingly their words touch your heart."

"Marko!" shrieked Yianoula.

"Above all, you must learn to love poetry, for this is what the miroloy is: a beautiful epic poem. When Hector was slain at Troy, Andromache sang his praises. And after she got tired, Hecuba took her place. She in turn was followed by Helen. They recounted Hector's battles, his victories, the way he held his shield, how he rode his horse, how he lived and died. This is the miroloy, my little flower. Without it, Greece could never have survived."

Yianoula was standing over him, both hands on her hips. "Are you through?"

Katina pulled her gently away. "Marko, I wish you would not say these things. Renio is too young."

"Death does not frighten the young," he said, leaning back on the couch.

Yianoula seized Renio's hand and pulled her to her feet.

"Where are you going?" said Marko.

"Home."

"But you just came."

"Yianoula, please do not go," Katina implored her. "Stay and eat with us."

"Yes," said Jason. "You must stay."

The anger in Yianoula's eyes melted. She walked to the

kitchen with Katina while Jason and his father played with Renio, asking her to close her eyes and tell them who was tickling her. Teasingly, Marko whispered to the child, "I can feel Him lurking out there."

"Who, Uncle Marko?"

"Charon."

"What does He look like? Have you ever seen Him?"

"Many times."

"Where?"

"Here in Livani, also in Kyparissia at my father's funeral."

"I want to see Him too."

"Be patient. In time we shall all see Him."

"Where does He live, Uncle Marko?"

"Far below the earth, under our very feet."

"At Taenarus?"

"Yes."

"I have been there many times but I never saw Him."

Marko put his finger to his lips. "He is a shrewd One and is very hard to find. But He knows each of us by name, even the color of our eyes and hair. You must not fear Charon, my little flower. Someday He will call out your name and then take you across a wide river into a sparkling new world where there is no pain, no burning sun, no bloated sheep. You will find many friends and relatives there; this is why you should not be afraid of Him."

"He does not frighten me, Uncle Marko."

"Good. Now then, go into the kitchen and help your Aunt Katina."

Jason followed the child into the kitchen and then opened the door to the porch.

"Where are you going?" asked his mother.

"Just for a short walk."

"In this heat?"

"I will not be gone long."

"Jason, have you taken leave of your senses?"

61

He climbed the high hill just behind the vineyard. From its summit he had an excellent view of Danae's house. He wondered what she was doing. He envisioned her moving around the small kitchen, ministering to her mother.

Above him, the sky was enflamed. And only a short time ago he had asked for this, dreading the long winter with its howling winds, craving to lie under the hottest rays of the sun.

He felt a sudden roll of thunder beneath his feet. Now another. Hurrying away from the hill, he raced through the vineyard as still one more roll echoed, louder and more frightening than the others. The earth started to pitch and heave, bending the olive trees, filling the air with dust, dislodging rocks from high places and sending them down the slopes of the hill. He shoved his body against the wall of a cliff and waited for the tremors to stop but the ground kept laboring and splitting open, swallowing rocks, trees, giant boulders.

He could not wait any longer. After a frantic rush across the yard, he threw himself into the house. Everyone was in the cellar. A lit taper was burning on top of an empty barrel. Yianoula was hugging Renio and weeping. His mother crossed herself when she saw him. "Thank God, you are safe," she murmured.

His father did not speak. Loud noises erupted overhead, things falling on the kitchen floor, windows breaking. The minutes dragged. Now silence.

"I think it has stopped," said Jason. He started up the cellar stairs.

"Wait a while longer," his father warned. "It could start again."

Jason restrained himself for another five minutes. He could not believe his eyes when he finally stepped outside. This was not his father's land, these mammoth boulders crushing the house and barn, the earth shattered in a thousand places, hot vapors steaming from the pores. Through the clouds of dust he saw Pavlo running toward him. "Friend Jason, where is my family?"

"They are safe," Jason assured him. "Everyone is safe."

Pavlo made the sign of the cross. "In the name of Zeus, I have never known an earthquake like this. Such terrifying noises! Are you certain no one was harmed?"

Jason grabbed him by the wrist.

"Where are we going?"

Jason's heart did not stop pounding until he saw Danae standing in front of her father's shop. Panos and his wife were clinging to each other at the door. Jason wanted to call out to her but just then she turned around and saw him. She clamped her hand over her mouth and crossed herself.

Pavlo was watching him. "Friend Jason, you disappoint me. I was always under the impression that you were an intelligent human being but now I have grave doubts."

"What do you mean?"

"You must be insane, getting involved with a girl from this village, strapping yourself to Livani forever. Open your eyes before it is too late!"

Jason pushed him away. Orestes' house was in shambles, one great pile of stones. The mandolin player was sitting on one of the slabs with Kyra Maria, their faces twitching, arms around each other. Across the street, a dozen men were digging at the ruins of Barba Manolis' house. The house of Pandelis the muleteer also lay in a heap. Dogs began to howl; roosters crowed.

More than half the village was demolished yet everyone was safe, even the animals. A deep crack extended along the façade of the church but amazingly not one window was broken. For the first time, Jason noticed that the bell tower was missing. It lay smashed in pieces on the dusty street.

An army of black clouds invaded the sky. The air turned cool. Flashes of lightning cut through the clouds and soon it started to rain.

Pavlo slapped his thigh in anger. "Friend God, first You dump Your load on us and now You want to flush it away!"

Jason was appalled. "Must you joke at a time like this?"

63

"Friend Jason, I am not joking. Lift up your eyes. There, do you see Him? Do you see God? In the name of Zeus, He is not a whiskered old man with a white dove perched on His head. God is a colossal bucket of water. Every time we stray or stumble or fall into sin, down He comes. But heaven help us on days like this when He Himself goes haywire. Friend Jason, God is not so difficult to find. See, I am soaked to the skin with Him. He is on my face, in my hair, inside my underwear. The old rascal is tickling my ass!"

2

Heads popped out of cellars, faces filled the streets, and from their midst arose Pappa Sotiri, his arms raised, his robe soaked. "On your knees, Christians! God has answered our prayers with His merciful rain. The drought has ended. On your knees!"

They did as the priest commanded, falling prostrate in the mud and crossing themselves. Jason alone remained standing, even after Pappa Sotiri approached and flashed his cross. "On your knees!" he exclaimed.

Jason turned sharply away from him, going first to Pandelis and pulling the muleteer to his feet. He went to Barba Manolis, Yeros Panayiotis, Orestes, Kyra Maria, Apostolis the salt-gatherer. "Who will take Pandelis?" he shouted to the kneeling crowd. "Who will give him bed and food until we build him another house?"

Someone raised his hand and soon a chorus of voices filled the sky. "Hey, Apostolis, you can stay with us! Alekos, bring your wife and your goats to our house! You there, Vasilis, gather up your family and come with us!"

No one was left homeless. They all got off their knees and,

with hands linked, walked through the mud and driving rain, past the incensed priest. "You had no right to do this!" he bellowed at Jason. "It is *my* duty to lead these people, not yours!"

Pavlo stepped between them. "Friend holiness, this is no time for a theological dispute. Come now, let my nephew alone. We must go home and attend to our families."

They were interrupted by a piercing cry from the church. A procession was coming toward them, four young men carrying a lifeless body on their shoulders.

"It is the idiot Fanoulis!" a woman screamed.

Jason shuddered. Pavlo tried to hold him back but he pushed him away and ran toward the cortege.

"The silly fool, he did not know enough to come down from the tower . . ."

"That is not true. I saw him running across the square at the first rumble. He wanted to ring the bell to warn us."

"The poor idiot!"

Orestes and Kyra Maria fought their way through the crowd and stopped at Jason's side. They both reached out to him, tears streaking down their faces, but he could not find one word to say to them.

"Is Fanoulis dead?" someone asked.

"Are you blind? Look at him."

Fanoulis' head was twisted to the side and dangling on the shoulder of a young bearer. The body was crushed, arms and legs bent into awkward angles. Kyra Maria threw herself into Orestes' comforting arms when a poisonous voice bellowed, "And who will sing the miroloy for Fanoulis?"

A wave of raucous laughter engulfed the square.

"The priest's wife, who else?"

"Eleni? She will never do it, not for that idiot!"

•   •

The wake was held at Jason's house that night. News of Fanoulis' death spread everywhere, even into the surrounding villages and hamlets. At first, the priest's wife rebelled when she was asked to sing the miroloy but she relented after the elders made a strong plea on behalf of Kyra Maria. "In the name of decency, she has been doctor and nurse to us for twenty-eight years!"

A large crowd had already gathered at the house well before dusk, cramming into every room. Dozens stood on the porch and in the yard waiting for the priest's wife. Jason wanted to chase them all away. It was turning into a circus. On the floor of the front room lay Fanoulis, a taper burning near his head, another at his feet. With whimpering tears, Kyra Maria kept telling everyone how she had to take a hammer to break Fanoulis' arms and legs in order to straighten them out until they lay flat. But she could do nothing about the face.

When Pappa Sotiri finally made his appearance, he went first to Orestes and Kyra Maria, and offered them a few words of solace. Swinging his censer over the corpse, he then plunged into a long incantation. Every time he crossed himself the crowd followed suit.

"Eleni is coming!" someone announced.

Proud and erect, the priest's wife sliced her way through the prying faces and walked straight to the corpse. Katina tried to hand her a lit taper but Eleni refused to take it. Her presence electrified the house. She was not a large woman but there was great strength in her eyes. In a voice cracking with embarrassment, she whispered to Katina, "I cannot do it. I cannot go through with this farce!"

"You must," said Katina soothingly. "If you falter, close your eyes and say to yourself, 'This is not Fanoulis. This is a fallen warrior, a hero who sacrificed his life for our village.'"

Eleni wrung her hands. "But look at that silly grin, those missing teeth. It *is* Fanoulis!"

The priest turned around and gave his wife a stern look. Sucking an exasperating breath, Eleni brought her hands behind her back and began unfolding her gray hair until it cascaded over her shoulders. A great hush filled the house. She grabbed two ends of her hair and wrapped them around her fingers. In a weird sawing motion, she tugged first with one hand then the other, pulling her head from side to side while the rest of her hair fell in wild disorder over her perspiring face. Her powerful voice shook the house. "Fanoulis, where are they taking you, my brave warrior? Can Charon not see how much we all need you? We shall be helpless without you. Who will sweep out Barba Manolis' taverna? Who will water his basil pots?"

A stream of laughter trickled through the house.

"Who will sound the church bell, brave Fanoulis? How will we know the difference between night and day? You are our sun and moon. We cannot live without you . . ."

"Po, po, po," muttered Yeros Panayiotis, who was standing next to Jason. "She is carving out thick slices again. Is this Fanoulis at our feet or is it Odysseus?"

The dirge continued for almost an hour. The laughter abated. Eleni rigidly kept her eyes away from the crowd and followed Pappa Sotiri out of the house. Eventually everything became quiet. Only a handful of people remained at Kyra Maria's side. "I tried not to listen when they laughed," she blurted out to them. "I said to myself, 'I should be grateful that they came.'"

"They can all go to hell!" bellowed Marko. He went to the cellar for more wine. Wiping her swollen eyes, Kyra Maria said to Jason, "Fanoulis always admired you. You never poked fun at him. Please do this one last thing for him."

"Of course," said Jason.

"Go to the priest tonight and ask him to bring out the grand lanterns for the funeral tomorrow. You were a soldier. He will listen to you."

Pavlo banged his fist on the table. "Friend midwife, do you have any idea what you are asking? The grand lanterns are only brought out for very special occasions—the death of a king, a prime minister, a patriarch!"

Kyra Maria broke into new sobs. "My son was a hero. He gave his life to Livani."

Pavlo flung up his hands and paced around the table. "I can tell you right now what goatbeard's answer will be!"

"If Jason wants to do it, let him," said Katina, with a stiff toss of her head.

"You are dreamers, all of you!"

Katina kissed the midwife. "Kyra Maria, you must try and get some sleep now. Tomorrow will be an arduous day."

"How can I sleep, Katina? Charon is lurking outside, waiting to take Fanoulis."

"We will stand watch over him."

"And I shall join you," declared Pavlo, throwing his arm around Orestes. "Friends of Hades, Fanoulis will be well-protected tonight. I promise you!"

•   •

It was a waste of time, pleading with the priest, asking him to bring out the grand lanterns. Pappa Sotiri wanted no part of it. *Do you take me for a fool? I will be the laughingstock of this village. No! A thousand times no!*" Jason did not have the heart to tell Kyra Maria.

Most of Livani was jammed inside the church the next morning. Jason was one of the first to arrive. He took a place directly in front of the iconostasis. His mother and father stationed themselves next to Orestes and Kyra Maria just behind the coffin. For the first time since Jason could remember, Fanoulis was not ringing the funeral bell.

The service started on time. Pappa Sotiri quietly slid open the door of the iconostasis and approached the coffin, swinging his censer and murmuring a hasty prayer. At his side stood two altar boys in black robes. Each held a lit taper in his hand, nothing else. Something burst inside Jason's brain. He dashed into the sanctuary and searched wildly for the grand lanterns. He found two of them leaning against the east wall near the window. He picked them up then came and stood beside the coffin. Pavlo left his place and seized one of the lanterns from Jason's hand, holding it high for everyone to see. The veins on Pappa Sotiri's neck swelled and threatened to explode.

Kyra Maria suddenly stopped weeping. Orestes lifted his head proudly, oblivious to the rolling heads and wagging tongues. Katina cast an admiring look toward Jason. The priest was too paralyzed to reprimand Jason and Pavlo. Stammering and choking, he sped through the service then led the procession out of the church and up the long hill to the cemetery. The presence of the grand lanterns weighed heavily on his sagging shoulders. His eyes kept flitting toward Jason and Pavlo, then toward the sky as though he expected God to strike them down for perpetrating such a comedy.

The procession passed through the open iron gate of the cemetery then stopped at the freshly dug grave. Once again Pappa Sotiri swung his censer over the coffin. Her eyes still gleaming, Kyra Maria stepped forward and exclaimed, "Sit up, my son. Open your sleepy eyes. Do you see the grand lanterns? Reach out, my Fanoulis. Feel their smooth golden faces!"

The women crossed themselves and craned their necks, waiting for the corpse to rise. One of the older men squeaked out a laugh. After several quick prayers, Pappa Sotiri gave a nervous signal to Aleko the sexton, and with the help of four young men the coffin was lowered into the shallow grave. The priest grabbed the grand lanterns and took flight. Tearfully, Kyra Maria dropped a white rose on the coffin then fell into Katina's arms.

Jason was the last to leave the cemetery. *Little Icarus, you will not be a child forever. Before you realize it, hair will grow on your face, under your armpits, around your groin. You will drink wine and ouzo, sleep with a woman, father her children; and then one day Charon will come and take you on a long journey across a deep river, into a strange and wonderful world* ...

Pavlo was waiting for him at the iron gate. "Friend Jason, that was a heroic thing you just did, confronting this whole damn village, that fat priest."

Jason kept walking.

"In the name of Zeus, wait. I want to ask you a special favor. After the last breath leaves my mouth, I want you to lift me on your shoulders and carry me to the highest peak of Taygetus. Do you understand?"

Jason lengthened his strides.

"In the name of Zeus, I want you to pay attention to me. It must be the tallest peak of Taygetus. I will be safe there because that cursed Cave-Dweller, Charon, is afraid of heights!"

3

He got up early the next morning and filled his haversack with bread and cheese, hard-boiled eggs, olives, a jar of lupine beans, a bottle of wine. Danae was standing outside the schoolyard, waiting for him. When she saw the haversack she asked him where they were going but he gave her no answer. He took her by the hand and they hurried across the square. At the north pass she asked once again.

"We should be there in a few hours," was his response.

"Jason, why are you so mysterious? Where are we going?"

"I will tell you later." He smiled.

They climbed up a high ridge terraced in ribs of stone. Prickly pear trees flourished in a small field. The air rattled with cicadas. Danae wanted to rest but he nudged her on, helping her up a high shelf of rock that brought them before a deep cave. It offered protection from the vicious wind. Jason took everything out of the haversack except the wine.

"Are you saving it for some reason?" Danae laughed teasingly.

He passed her a chunk of cheese. "Yes, for the goatherd. It was he who first showed me the place."

"What place?"

He avoided her question. They sat and ate in silence. After a few moments, he stood up. "We still have a hard climb before us."

They wedged their way through a high gorge. Great birds soared in the sky. They stopped and drank from a small pool of water then moved toward a bleached plateau that rose above them. No matter where they stood, the immovable face of Taygetus glared down at them. Jason's eyes kept searching the rocks for the goatherd but he was nowhere in sight.

"Jason, I am getting tired."

"We cannot stop again. We are losing the sun."

"Please, only for a little while."

He reached for her hand. It was cold. He pulled her into his arms and kissed her on the lips, the neck. His hand found her breast but she pushed it away.

"What is the matter?" he said.

"Jason, why did you bring me up here?"

He pulled her close once more but she wrestled out of his arms. "I will not climb another step unless you tell me!" she exclaimed.

He pointed toward the distant peaks. "There, just above that sharp precipice, can you see the red tiles?"

She shook her head.

"It is a monastery."

"You brought me all the way up here just to look at a monastery?"

"Come closer. Do you see those tiny white specks below

the precipice? That is the village of Akra. The goatherd lives there."

"Jason, I want to go back."

"But we just got here."

"I do not like this place. Please, let us go back."

He was not listening to her. '*My little Icarus, God is a breath, an inaudible whisper that can push back mountains, split open the sea, fill the fathomless void of the universe . . .*'

She fell into his arms, clutching him with all her strength. He wanted to take her, there on the rocky cliff, under the shadow of God's breath. He tried to fight it but the warmth of her body kept enticing him. In desperation, he eased her down then fumbled with his trousers. Embracing her once again, he felt her arms stiffen. "There is nothing to fear," he whispered. Her arms relaxed but not completely. He was inside her now, slowly, deeply—spurred by her gasping breath on his ear, her moistness, her soft thighs.

There was a voice at the door of his brain. Refusing to listen, he clamped his eyes shut and kept thrusting, thrusting, but the voice was relentless: *Foolish Jason, is this what you want, or is it Athens? You cannot have both!*

Banging his fists on the rock, he quickly withdrew and allowed his burning seed to spill over the ground.

4

His body ached with fatigue that night. He ate very little. His mother cleared the table and washed the dishes then went to call on Yianoula. Alone with his father, Jason felt uneasy and restless. Finally something goaded him to say, "Did you ever think about leaving this village . . ."

"Why do you ask?" grunted Marko.

"I cannot understand your great love for this place. You have nothing to your name but those gnarled olive trees. They have imprisoned you, stripped you of all identity, and yet you cling to them. Why?"

"Someday you will know," said Marko.

"I think Pavlo is right. We should all abandon this cursed land and go to America."

Marko started pacing around the table.

"We still have time," said Jason. "It is not too late to free ourselves."

"What the hell do you know about freedom?" cried Marko, clenching his fists. "I will never be free. Neither will you!"

"That is not true."

"We are all trapped, Athenian, every last one of us—the living as well as the dead."

Jason shook his head vehemently.

In a rush of anger, Marko grabbed the bread knife from the table and ran its sharp edge over his thumb until blood spurted out. "This keeps us from being free," he shouted, thrusting the thumb in front of Jason's face. "Do not turn your eyes away. Look here. These are your ancestors, each pulsating drop. You cannot hide from them. No matter where you go, Athens, Salonika, America, they will always be inside you!"

"Is this why you have never left?"

"Yes."

"Because of them?"

"Yes."

Jason pushed back his chair and stood up. "Can you not see it?" he said. "You have given in to your fears. Our ancestors have no control over us. We alone determine our fate."

"You are a fool," shouted Marko. He slammed his fist on the table, opening the wound and sending a blotch of blood over the white tablecloth. Just then Jason's mother returned to the house. She raced to the closet and brought back a towel but Marko flung it away.

"In the name of the Virgin," she exclaimed. "What did

you do to yourself? I wish you would stop drinking when you are tired. Get away from the table and go to bed."

Marko obeyed. At the door of the bedroom he stopped and turned around. "Do you see what I mean, Athenian? No one is free!"

After a while his mother too retired for the night. He paced around the kitchen floor for a long time and then slumped into his chair. His father's words still bothered him. He tried to think of happier moments. He remembered the first time he went to Kalamata with his father. He was seven years old. The olive groves had given them a plentiful harvest. He would never forget that clear cold morning in December, born from a night of nagging rain, his mother running from the house to wave goodbye, and he, trembling with joy, waving back to her. They took the inland road. The mare jogged leisurely along, swaying her hips and swishing her tail. Jason bubbled with joy. "Faster, Bouboulina. Faster," he commanded, catching the proud glance from his father's eye. The ungainly mare seemed to respond and she pranced forward on her knobby legs, her large ears drooping over her eyes, her bony rear quarters listing to and fro. But she covered ground, and when they came in sight of the old fortress outside Kalamata, his father pulled up on the reins and pointed to the ancient stones. His great-grandmother had sacrificed her life there, she and hundreds of Greeks. The Turk did not frighten her. She stood on that citadel and fought to the death. Later, when they were inside Kalamata, Jason heard a thunderous noise behind him. The mare reared back and bolted down the street. The sudden appearance of the train had terrified Jason also but when he saw his father laughing he too laughed and was no longer afraid.

•   •

The season of wine-making. Sleepless Boreas howling over the Peloponnesus, scouring the earth for his loved-one Orithyia.

74

Livani never changing. The same old faces, narrow streets, and tight little houses; the same pinched sky.

Jason helped his father pick all the grapes, carry them into the cellar, empty them into the press. The thick juice had started dripping into the large wooden tub under the press when Pavlo came down the cellar stairs. "Friends of the vineyard, I caught this heavenly aroma drifting all the way into my kitchen."

"Boreas was gnawing at my insides," said Marko.

Pavlo tasted the juice with his fingers. "Friend of the grape, you need not explain. I am not on speaking terms with that vile wind either—but this is the price we must pay for living in this labyrinth. But it will not be long. Jason and I will soon be on our way to America, opening the door of freedom for all of us." He leaned over the press and put his fingers into the juice again. "Mmm, it is beyond speech."

Marko laughed. He seemed relaxed and happy. Jason remembered that he was always this way during the wine season. It did not take much, a crushed grape, the heavy scent permeating the cellar.

Jason turned the wheel with him and when the last grape was crushed they strained the juice into a clean barrel. Taking the wooden stopper, Marko plugged the hole then poured melted wax over it. Before it hardened, he engraved a sign of the cross with his finger.

"May it become good wine," said Pavlo. "May we drink it on Christmas Day."

"Christmas seems centuries away," muttered Marko.

"Where can it hide? Before you know it we shall be hearing the carols. Friend nephew, why so quiet? I am glad to see you helping your father but you look troubled. What is it?"

Jason had his eyes fastened on the engraved cross. "I was thinking about God . . ."

"Did you say God? Perhaps it is time we all thought about Him. I am not referring to that bearded old man who sits on a golden throne with a weak-kneed son on his right hand and a winged mother on his left. It is unworthy of us to worship that kind of God. The true God is a camera. We curse, click. We lie, click. We cheat, click. We commit adultery, click, click, click! Nothing escapes the eye of that camera. When that ill-fated day comes and Charon carries us across the river Styx we shall be separated from the sheep and goats not by Saint Peter but by the camera. In the name of Argus, it will play back everything: click, click, click!"

Jason picked up an empty crate and sat down.

"Friends of the vineyard, let us carry this thing a bit further. I say that it is a good thing to be curious about life. This is the only way we can learn."

"We never learn," said Marko, wiping his hands on a coarse towel. "We keep making the same mistakes from youth to old age."

Pavlo snickered. "What do you know about old age?"

"I know enough to accept it when it comes, something you will never learn," snapped Marko.

Pavlo flung up his hands. "What is it about Greeks? They turn every discussion into a personal argument. In the name of Zeus, all I am trying to say is that many things should stir our curiosity. For example, we must stop regarding woman as nothing more than a machine for making babies."

Jason got up from the crate and started to leave but Pavlo stopped him. "Friend nephew, does this offend you? Man too is a machine. If we could take one look at our insides we would see miles of tubes twisting through our bodies. We must feed these tubes, give them drink, watch over them every moment otherwise they will get rusty and deteriorate. A woman's tubes have different functions, different needs. Let me ask you something, why are we repeatedly warned to keep away from women during holy days?"

Jason tried to move around him but Pavlo blocked his path. "I can see through these devilish schemes. The goatbeards want to castrate us. When this happens, women will rule the earth, women and goatbeards! Let me give you another example, on the night of my wedding . . ."

"We already know about it," said Marko.

"I am not speaking about the sheets. This is another matter. And therefore, I could see that something was troubling my new wife. As for myself, I was concerned only about the bed. After that mad family left, I undressed slowly so as not to alarm Yianoula, but no sooner did I crawl into bed beside her when she threw the covers off and ran to the small icon shelf near the door. Right before my eyes, she took a piece of cloth and carefully covered the Virgin's face. And why? Because she did not want the Virgin to see what we were about to do. This is what I mean about goatbeards. Once they leave their mark on you it can never be erased."

"You are full of shit," said Jason laughing. This time he eluded Pavlo's grasp and started for the cellar stairs. Pavlo came running after him. "You must listen to me. The goatbeards want to make the Virgin their queen. We shall be their slaves. But it is not too late. We can still save ourselves. Friend nephew, why are you sneaking off like that?"

Marko went to the barrel of juice and turned the spigot. He took a long drink then stepped aside for Pavlo to have his turn.

"To God the camera!" Pavlo exclaimed, wiping his mouth with the back of his hand.

Jason lingered at the top of the stairs, watching and listening to them.

"Friends of Bacchus, I have a serious question to ask you."

"What is it?" said Marko.

"I am gravely concerned about my nephew, my sister's son."

"What do you mean?"

"I think we both should go to Panos and warn him to keep that nereid away from Jason."

"What nereid?"

"The poor cobbler has a sick wife on his hands. Who will

77

take care of the unfortunate woman if the nereid marries Jason?"

"What the hell are you talking about?"

"In the name of Zeus, are you blind? The whole village knows about them."

"Jason and the cobbler's daughter?"

"I already have had one talk with Jason about this matter. If he is not careful he will be doomed, imprisoned in her grotto forever, and he will never come to America with me."

Marko took another drink from the spigot.

"I hope it is not too late," Pavlo went on. "But I am afraid. Have you noticed the way Jason has been walking these past few weeks? It is not a virgin's walk."

Playfully, Pavlo shoved Marko away from the spigot and helped himself to a long drink but Marko fought back and after he had one final gulp they stood there laughing at each other, their faces stained, their shirts soaked.

"The spigot," cried Marko. "You forgot to turn it off!"

"Let it run, friend of the virgin. My forgiven mother always said it was a good omen when wine spilled."

Jason quietly closed the cellar door.

5

At the supper table that night he told his parents that he had altered his plans and would not leave for Athens until the fall. His mother was overjoyed and several times she tried to say something to him but tears clogged her throat. His father showed no emotion but after a while he narrowed his eyes and asked, "What made you change your mind?"

Jason could not tell him that he was torn between Athens and Danae, one minute wanting desperately to escape from

Livani, and the next, dreading the thought of losing her. And there was Pavlo, hounding him constantly about America, never relenting. Jason had refused to take him seriously before but now everything was different.

He slept fitfully that night. In the morning he met Danae at the quay. She looked upset. He asked her what was troubling her but she did not answer. Only after they returned from a long walk along the shore did she finally speak. "I am going to Athens with my mother."

"When?" he asked.

"Tomorrow morning."

"For what reason?"

"My father wants a specialist to examine her. We should be back in a week or so . . ."

Those were her last words, and now three weeks had gone by. Every morning he walked past her father's cobbler shop, tempted to go inside and ask Panos when they would be returning from Athens. On the fourth week he sank into a deep melancholy.

"Jason, is anything ailing you?" his mother asked one night at the supper table.

He shook his head.

"Perhaps it is your navel . . ."

He pushed back his chair and fled outside. At least once each year throughout his childhood Kyra Maria would stretch him out on the kitchen floor, dab her thick forefinger into a small dish of warm olive oil, shove it into his navel, press down hard then make three full turns, stopping at certain intervals to emit some mystical words. The pain tormented him but both Kyra Maria and his mother maintained that his navel had gotten loose and needed tightening, otherwise he would go through life weak and sickly, unable to eat, a skeleton. All the navels in Livani and his alone kept getting loose!

Not knowing what to do with himself, he went to the

church the next morning. Pappa Sotiri had just finished with matins and was arranging his gold vessels on the holy table.

"Your holiness, I would like to speak to you."

"What is it?" The priest glared at him.

"I wanted to tell you this weeks ago but I could not find the courage."

"Speak. What are you trying to say?"

"That I am sorry . . ."

"For what?"

"I did not intend to humiliate you that day of the earthquake, and also the next day at the funeral with the grand lanterns. Something came over me which I cannot explain. Please forgive me."

Pappa Sotiri's eyes melted. He lifted his hand and blessed him then turned to the gold vessels once again.

"Did you know there is a monastery high in the mountains, just beyond Akra?" said Jason.

"Of course."

"I climbed there recently."

The priest spun around. "You went to the monastery?"

"No. I reached a place in the mountains where I could see it clearly. It looked beautiful, so peaceful and beautiful."

Pappa Sotiri crossed himself. "How I longed to go there when I was a young man, to spend the rest of my life in quietude, free from noise and sin!" He attached his eyes to the icon of Saint Chrysostomos and groaned. "But God had other plans for me."

"If you had gone to the monastery what would you have sought?" said Jason.

The priest cleared his throat. "There are many reasons why a man enters a monastery. He can always expect to find food on the table. Does this shock you? Escape is another reason. He can find asylum from the cruel demands of life by losing his identity until nothing remains but an acute awareness of God. But why did you ask this question? Surely you are not thinking of entering a monastery?"

Jason laughed nervously.

Pappa Sotiri's voice became serious. "The life of a monk is an eternal struggle. He must first adjust to the terrible truth that he is different from other men, that he will never eat meat again, nor touch a woman, even in his thoughts; that he must separate himself from family, friends, loved ones; absorb himself entirely in prayer and meditation."

Jason wanted to hear more but he suddenly remembered that he had to get to the quay before all the fish were sold. Pappa Sotiri was reluctant to stop. He gathered his vestments together and accompanied him down the steps of the church. "Perhaps we can continue this at some other time."

Jason nodded.

The priest lifted his hand and blessed him once again. "It is impossible to find absolute answers in this insane world. If you want to be happy you must love God, honor your parents, marry, have children, work . . ."

'And die!' cried Jason under his breath. He bade the priest goodbye and ran toward the quay. The caïques had already rounded the gulf and were gliding into the harbor. He arrived just in time. A suntanned fisherman took his ten drachmas and threw a half-dozen fish into a newspaper. Jason wrapped them up carefully and walked away. When he came into the square he caught sight of Danae standing outside her father's shop. She ran to greet him. "Jason, I have been looking for you!"

"When did you get back from Athens?" he asked. He could feel his heart fluttering.

"Just about an hour ago. I am so glad to see you!"

He wanted to take her into his arms. "Why were you gone so long?"

She took hold of his free arm and squeezed it.

"Danae, how is your mother?"

"I have wonderful news, Jason. The specialist found nothing wrong with her!"

"I am glad to hear it," he said.

Her eyes flashed. "I have yet to answer you why we stayed in Athens so long."

"Why?"

"I applied to the University . . ."

"What?"

"My mother encouraged me to take the examinations. I could not believe it, but from the moment the specialist told her there was nothing wrong with her, she changed. She is a totally different person. Do you know what this means, Jason? We can be in Athens together!"

He stopped walking. "Will I see you tonight?" he asked coldly.

Her eyes were hurt. Before she could answer, the door of the cobbler shop swung open and Panos stepped outside. He smiled when he saw them. Wiping the perspiration from his face with the back of his hand, he said, "What is that you are carrying, Jason?"

"I bought some fish at the quay," Jason stammered. He felt very uncomfortable talking to Panos. He bade them both a quick goodbye and started down the street. In front of the church he came to a sudden stop. Something felt warm and moist against his chest. Looking down, he discovered the newspaper had split open, staining his shirt with blood.

●　　　●

It rained that night, a hard downpour that struck Livani with such intensity he had to postpone any thought of seeing Danae. Tossing an oilskin over his head, he ran to the taverna. It was crammed with the usual faces, Pavlo holding forth as chief jester. He treated Jason to a glass of wine then went back to his table. Through the half-open door Pappa Sotiri's voice carried into the taverna:

> *Lord, I cry unto Thee,*
> *Make haste,*
> *Give ear to my voice . . .*

Pavlo put down his glass and slapped his thigh. "Listen to that goatbeard. I ask you, is this a vesper service? In the name of Justinian, let me sing you a real Byzantine chant. Ne, ti, ri, rem!"

Barba Manolis blocked up his ears, and from the adjacent table Yeros Panayiotis giggled, but Pavlo chanted on, "Ne, ti, ri, rem—ti, ri, rem!"

"Stop that nonsense," cried Barba Manolis, snapping his wet apron against the table. "This is a place of business!"

"Friend of the coffee grounds, what you just heard is a pure Byzantine chant, not nonsense."

"You sound like a sick Turk."

Pavlo filled all the glasses at the table then walked over to Jason and filled his. Looking toward Barba Manolis, he said, "I am knocking at the door of a deaf man. I am tickling the foot of a corpse."

"What the hell does that mean?" shouted Barba Manolis.

"He who has ears, let him listen. The camel never sees its own hump."

Jason moved to one of the tables in the far corner of the taverna and began reading a newspaper. Yeros Panayiotis spotted him and came to sit beside him. "What is the news today?" he chuckled. "Has Hitler pissed yet? Did Mussolini take a shit?"

Jason carefully put down the newspaper. "Mussolini is doing his utmost to goad us into a war. His airplanes are harassing our ships in the Aegean, and only yesterday one of his submarines torpedoed and sank the Greek cruiser *Helle*."

"Where did this happen?"

"Off the island of Tinos."

Yeros Panayiotis started to weep and Pavlo came running to the table. "Friend nephew, what did you say to this old man? Why is he crying?"

"He cries over everything," snorted Barba Manolis. "I cannot understand why God created old men. They are good for nothing, utterly useless!"

Yeros Panayiotis kept at it.

Barba Manolis lost his patience. He bent over the old man and shook him hard with both hands. "Stop that. This is a place of business!"

Pavlo pushed Barba Manolis away. "Coffee-grinder, what makes you think this is a place of business? Take a good look. These people are sitting here for only one reason, to be educated. Where do you think Socrates was educated? In the University of Athens? Look there, toward Master Theophilos. He is the lighthouse of our village, the teacher of Livani. He too comes here to be educated. Is this not so, Master Theophilos?"

The old teacher nodded his head several times. Pavlo came beside him and filled his glass with more wine as Jason picked up the newspaper.

"Continue. Continue," croaked Yeros Panayiotis.

Jason put the newspaper down. "What more can I tell you? It is the same news day after day, German planes bombing England, the British retaliating with heavy raids on Berlin, Düsseldorf, Essen, more Jews taken to concentration camps and burned in ovens."

"I think the world is coming to an end," said Master Theophilos.

"The British houses of parliament are badly damaged," Jason went on. "London is in shambles. I do not think the English people can endure the destruction much longer."

Yeros Panayiotis raised his cane. "I predict . . ."

"I told you to stop predicting," said Pavlo. "No one can predict anything."

"Christ did."

"Who?"

"Jesus Christ. He predicted that Jerusalem would be totally destroyed, not one stone left upon the other."

"That is what the Bible says."

"Do you not believe the Bible?" asked Yeros Panayiotis.

84

"I believe it when it says *Kyrie eleison* and *Amen*, but not when it tries to tell me that Christ walked on the Sea of Galilee, or that He fed five thousand people with two loaves of bread."

"You are a heretic!" exclaimed Yeros Panayiotis.

Jason pushed away the newspaper and stood up.

"Where are you going?" said Pavlo.

"Nowhere. I am only stretching my legs."

A short while later, after vespers came to an end, Jason went to a table near the window and sat down. Pavlo joined him. A half-dozen women were coming down the church steps, their heads bent, fighting the wind and rain. When Pavlo spotted the priest he ran out of the taverna and brought him inside. Pappa Sotiri scanned the tables with angry eyes then shook his robe, sending a spray over Jason.

"Sit down, your holiness," said Pavlo. "Join us for a glass of wine."

Pappa Sotiri wiped his face with a napkin and sat beside Jason.

"A wine for his holiness," Pavlo called out to Barba Manolis in the back room.

The priest lifted his hands in protest. "I prefer a coffee, medium-sweet."

"A medium-sweet for his holiness!"

"I heard you," responded Barba Manolis.

Pavlo brought his chair close to the priest. "And how did vespers go tonight, your holiness?"

Pappa Sotiri's face became taut. "I will never understand what induced God to create a Greek. Look at yourselves, sitting here on your lean bottoms, drinking, smoking, cursing, playing cards, and arguing while your saintly women pray for your detestable souls!"

Pavlo interrupted him. "Friend holiness, the greatest prayer in the world is a woman's tear. Did they not teach you this in the seminary?"

The priest ranted on. "I am a pastor without a flock. For twenty-nine years I have eaten your crumbs, condoned your ignorance, closed my eyes to your sins. Far worse, I have buried my talents under the bushel of darkness and obscurity."

Pavlo picked up the bottle of wine and poured a glass for him. "Friend holiness, you need something stronger than coffee tonight. Here, drink this wine. It will warm your heart with forgiveness. After all, Livani is not such a bad place. We may irritate you at times but do not forget that we also have provided you with a bed, a warm house, food on the table."

Pappa Sotiri gulped down the wine and did not object when Pavlo refilled his glass. "What have I to show for my sixty-eight years? My pockets are empty, I beg for your food, I am childless. Every morning I stand before the mirror and ask myself: 'Why were you born? What have you accomplished in life? You are a cipher, a cipher.'"

Jason saw tears in the priest's eyes. "Come, your holiness, let me walk you home."

"Take your hands off me!"

Pavlo filled Pappa Sotiri's glass for the third time. "Bravo, friend holiness, this is no time for sleep. I was just about to begin a serious discussion." He leaped on his chair and clapped his hands. "Friends of the earth and outer planets, look about you. Can you honestly find one person who is of sound mind? Just one? We are all being devoured by a universal insanity. Sons detest fathers, daughters envy mothers, families hate families, nations fight nations. In the name of Zeus, where are we going? Speak up, friend holiness. Tell us why God hides His face from all this!"

"He has no face," declared Barba Manolis, approaching their table with the priest's coffee. Pavlo pushed it aside with the back of his hand, spilling some on Barba Manolis' apron.

"That is correct," said the priest in a giddy voice. "God is a pure spirit and as such He has no face."

86

"He is pure goatshit," exclaimed Barba Manolis.

The priest was horrified. "Why do you speak like this?"

"Because He destroyed my house!"

Pappa Sotiri took a sip of the coffee. "Are you trying to say that God is responsible for that earthquake?"

"Who else? Can you produce an earthquake?"

The priest stood up.

"Your holiness, you cannot leave now," said Pavlo. "I was just about to tell everyone about Theotokis . . ."

"That idiot!" cried Barba Manolis, walking away. Yeros Panayiotis jabbed his cane at the floor and fell into a fit of laughter. Pavlo silenced him. "Yes, Theotokis had a feeble brain as we all know but God judges the heart. I remember the day when Theotokis announced he would run for mayor. We tried to reason with him, begged him to withdraw his name but we were talking to the wind. If you recall, Theotokis was endowed with a harelip. And there we were, friends of Greece, in the middle of this political campaign! Naturally we banded around Theotokis but our votes were few and we lost. That night the opposing forces converged upon Theotokis' house and in the spirit of a Greek election began mocking and deriding him. 'Speech! Speech!' they clamored. We implored him not to show his face but he did not listen. Walking boldly to his balcony, he raised his hands and cried: 'Are you all here?' 'Yes! Yes!' they responded. 'Are you thure no one ith mithing?' 'No one!' they exclaimed. 'Then I thit on you. I thit on every latht one of you!' "

The priest blew into his handkerchief to keep from laughing. Pavlo filled all the glasses once more and after another round he ordered a bottle of retsina.

"What is the occasion?" growled Barba Manolis.

"Retsina is more appropriate for a philosophical discussion," answered Pavlo, pacing around the tables. "Friends of the Lyceum, allow me to change the subject for a moment. Just this morning, after leading my goats to pasture, I stopped beside a laurel bush, begging your pardon, to relieve myself. When I finished, I looked down at the mess I had just created and said, 'Friend shit, you were such a delicious meal last night: heavenly slices of tomato, white feta cheese, eggs and olives, bread, wine. But look at yourself now. In the name of Dionysus, you stink so badly I cannot come near you!' "

"Must you talk about shit in front of the priest?" Jason admonished him.

"Friend nephew, we are involved in a serious matter here. Hold your tongue and listen. As I was saying, friends of the Lyceum, we must have the courage to ask ourselves what mysterious force can transform an innocent little olive into a stinking mess of shit. Let us philosophize for a moment. It is my theory that after God created the world He gorged Himself on food and drink. Consequently, He had to rest on the seventh day because He was drunk, happy but drunk. In the middle of the night He felt a desperate need to relieve Himself, and so, He took a shit, called it man, commanded it to multiply and stink up the earth. Thus ends the gospel according to Pavlo. Ne, ti, ri, rem—ti, ri, rem!"

The priest was slouched over the table, snoring. Pavlo tossed an impatient nod to Barba Manolis. "Take the goatbeard home."

"*You* made him drunk. *You* take him home."

"I sleep with your ancestors!"

"And I sleep with your mangy goats!"

One of the young men volunteered to take the priest home while Jason helped Pavlo out of the taverna. The rain had stopped; stars were flickering in the warm night. "Friend nephew, you cannot hide it from me any longer. Answer me truthfully. Have you been plucking the feathers of that juicy bird in Panos' yard?"

Jason ignored him.

"If you have, you had better put an end to it. And what is all this business about you and the priest? Why do you keep seeing him? Is he brainwashing you, trying to turn you into a goatbeard? For the last time, I implore you to unbuckle yourself from this horrible village; sever yourself completely from that nereid, from priests and monasteries. Time is slipping through our fingers, friend Jason. America cannot wait forever!"

THREE

The swift death of August. The taverna every night despite his mother's tearful pleas, sinking deeper into the labyrinth, wanting Danae yet seeking other answers, elusive, drifting on gossamer wings above the gray stones of a monastery. And Pavlo, always coming back to Pavlo, allowing him to fill his mind with new hope, with visions of freedom and flight. He hated himself when he returned home in the early hours of morning, his breath reeking from wine and cigarettes, his eyes smarting. His mother waited for him in the kitchen no matter how late it was, pouring out her anguish, beseeching him to come to his senses. His father never said a word. Marko often visited the taverna but he seldom stayed. He drank a few glasses of wine then left, avoiding all discussions and political arguments.

Jason continued to help him in the groves. Most of the preparation for the harvest was completed. Never before had the olive trees produced a more bountiful crop.

Late one afternoon he took Danae for a long walk into the hills and from the moment they left the village she did not say a word.

"Is something troubling you?" he asked.

She kept her eyes on the ground.

"Danae, what is it? Why are you acting like this?"

"I am concerned about my mother. She has not been feeling well. She is always tired and has no appetite for food."

"Perhaps it is not serious," he said. "She may have caught a chill."

"My father is worried about her."

"But she told you in Athens that the specialist found nothing wrong with her. There is no need for you and your father to worry. Has Kyra Maria looked at her?"

"Kyra Maria has gone to visit her sister in Kalamata. She will not be back for another week."

"This should convince you," said Jason. "Kyra Maria would never have left if she thought your mother's condition was serious."

"Something else has been troubling me, Jason."

"What is it?"

"I have yet to receive word from the University."

"You must be patient. These things take time. You are not the only one who took examinations."

"I will die if they do not accept me."

"Stop worrying about things that will never happen," he said. He came closer and took her into his arms, holding her tightly until she stopped trembling. "Perhaps we should head back," he said.

She nodded.

They took a different path through a long corridor of rocks and down a sharp hill. The once-vibrant laurel patches were drying out. The oleanders had completely lost their color. At the bottom of the hill she stopped and looked at him. "Jason, when are you going to Athens?"

He forced a laugh. "Do you want me to go?"

"I would rather have you go than see you like this."

"Like what?"

She continued walking. "Jason, you have never told me what you want to do, really want to do."

He listened to the wind.

Shadows were already cloaking the feet of Taygetus. When they entered the village, he suddenly swung around. "I know what I want to do. Why did I not think about it sooner? Now that Fanoulis is dead I will take his place. I will climb to the tower of the church every day and ring the bell. I will ring

94

it so loud everyone in the Peloponnesus will hear it. This will be my future. I shall go to the tower right now and begin!"

"Jason!"

He pushed her aside and ran across the street to the church. The front door was open. When he got to the tower he seized the rope and started pulling. Heads popped out of windows and doors, children came running into the street, dogs howled. He was obsessed. Sweat poured down his face, his arms ached, his head spun from the deafening concussions.

Breathless and shaking, he finally stopped. He was met by a surging tide of faces in the street. He could not tell if they were angry or amused. Danae had disappeared. Moving rapidly through the dense crowd, he was overwhelmed by a strange sensation. Something deep inside him had freed itself. Lighter than the wind, invisible, it was already soaring effortlessly and with exhilarating speed into the heart of the autumn sun.

2

Kostaki ambled into the taverna that night as though he had never been away—Kostaki who had gone to Athens to become a rich man, back again in Livani with only a few drachmas to his name. Jason was overjoyed to see him. They drank and smoked, returned to their schooldays, reminisced about the two years in the Reserves, laughed when they recalled how they took turns with Marigo, the cavernous widow of the village.

Kostaki's thin hands fidgeted with every memory, every word. The constant cigarette dangled from his lips. "Have you been screwing anyone?" he asked.

"Sure." Jason laughed.

"You look all shriveled up. I mean it, have you been screwing anyone?"

"Anyone and everyone."

Kostaki burped. "Who can you screw in this damn village except the widow Marigo?"

"What about you?" said Jason.

Kostaki shoved both hands over his crotch. "Every night. Bang, bang!"

"I do not believe you."

"It is the truth. In Athens I was getting it at least twice a day, sometimes more. Athens is not Livani. I have been here only one day and already I am out of practice. What do you say, let us go to Kalamata tomorrow. I know someone . . ."

"Kostaki, why did you come back?"

There was no response.

"Answer me, why did you come back to Livani?"

"I will tell you some other time."

"I want to know now," Jason persisted.

"There are other things to talk about."

"Like what?"

"It looks as though we are going to have a war. This is what everyone in Athens is saying. Do you think they could be right?"

"Kostaki, why are you dodging my question?"

"What question?"

"I want to know why you came back to Livani."

"Christ and the Virgin, what kind of welcome is this? I have only been here a few hours and you are picking me to pieces."

"I want to hear your answer."

"There you go again. I already told you that I cannot explain it now."

"Why not?"

"Because I am not in the mood."

"Then I will wait until you get into the mood."

"You may have to wait forever." Kostaki scowled. He walked away to another table and treated everyone there to a round of drinks. Jason sat alone for a while but he was soon joined by Pavlo. He was red with anger. "Friend nephew, I am sick and tired of the cackling hens in this place. I do not want to hear another word about politics. I do not give a damn about Mussolini or Hitler, Roosevelt or Churchill. In the name of Zeus, can we not talk about something else for a change?"

"Like what?" said Kostaki, coming back to Jason's table with a bottle of wine.

"Like the evil eye."

Barba Manolis stopped what he was doing and exclaimed, "When are we going to liberate ourselves from such pagan superstitions? Only children and old women believe in the evil eye!"

From an adjacent table, Yeros Panayiotis waited for silence then said, "When I was a young student in Sparta I saw an old man walking toward me one day. He was deathly pale. His clothes were worn to a frazzle and his body smelled so bad I could not come near him. 'Grandfather,' I said, 'why are you so downcast?' Without lifting his head, he answered, 'I am a cursed man. God, who is so merciful to others, has made me the most unhappy creature in the world. He endowed me with an eye that brings evil no matter where it rests.' I was young in heart those days and I did not believe in such primitive nonsense. This is exactly what I told the old man but it made no impression on him. Throughout our conversation, he continued to keep his eyes away from me. 'I cannot look at you,' he explained, 'because I do not want you to fall into a seizure and die!' Of course I laughed, but he meant it. 'You must believe me. I am really endowed with this power. Do you see that innocent little sparrow, there on that olive branch? If it turns its head and meets my eye it will fall to the ground dead. Please understand that I do not want to harm it. I just have to prove to you that I am powerless to prevent it.' Well, my children, that poor little sparrow turned its head and looked directly into the eyes of the old man, and that same instant, it toppled from the olive branch. I ran to pick it up but it was lifeless."

Pavlo shifted his attention to Stephanos the barber. "Speak up, friend of the scissors. Tell them what you told me about the evil eye."

Stephanos never changed—hair always smooth and wet, mustache neatly trimmed. Every aromatic scent from the bottles in the barber shop permeated his body. "When I was eighteen I journeyed with my father into a small village just to the north of Corinth. As you all know, my father was a puppeteer who traveled extensively throughout the Peloponnesus. He took me with him many times because he wanted me to learn his craft . . ."

"Get on with it," said Pavlo. "Tell them about the eye."

"We arrived in that village early one Sunday morning and my father insisted that we go to church. As you all know, he was a deeply religious man . . ."

"In the name of Zeus, tell them about the eye!"

"We sat next to a man with a dark mysterious face. During the entire service he kept staring at the floor. My father nudged him politely on the shoulder and said, 'Lift up your eyes. The priest is at the altar, not in the cellar!' The man nodded his head but he kept his eyes on the floor. 'I have the evil eye,' he said. 'If I look upon the priest or anyone else they will fall down and die.' 'You are crazy,' said my father, and with this he reached over and pulled the man's head up until the eyes finally opened and focused on the huge chandelier hanging down from the dome. At that very instant the chandelier broke away from its bolts and came crashing down on the floor. Fortunately no one was hurt. I saw this with my very own eyes. I swear!"

Jason broke into a laugh.

"It happened exactly as I told you," cried Stephanos, crossing himself.

"Then what prevented the floor from caving in?"

"The floor?"

"You said this man kept staring at the floor. If he was truly possessed by the eye the floor should have caved in too."

Several of the young men laughed. Pavlo got annoyed. "Friend nephew, the eye works only when it is provoked. Stop grinning. The ancients too feared it. This is what destroyed Oedipus and Agamemnon. It will destroy us also if we mock it and refuse to believe in it."

Jason lit another cigarette. Pavlo spun his chair around and turned to the priest, "Your holiness, certainly you believe in the evil eye?"

Pappa Sotiri crossed himself and cried, "I do not!"

"How about the church?"

"She does not believe in it either."

"Then why does she provide us with a special prayer to combat it?"

Pappa Sotiri squinted nervously. "In her divine wisdom, she uses these antidotes to quell our fears."

"One lie to wipe out another," snarled Barba Manolis.

The priest reprimanded him. "The church does not lie. Even from ancient times Greeks have loved to wallow in fear and superstition. The church acknowledges this and therefore employs the proper measures."

Pavlo laughed. "A quick *Kyrie eleison*, and now pick up your bed and walk!"

Pappa Sotiri silenced the laughter. "The church is God's warehouse. Every truth uttered from the beginning of time is stored in her bosom."

"She also stores a few untruths, your holiness. My mind works very slowly and needs oiling every so often. If the evil eye is nothing but superstition, why ask God to deal with it?"

Orestes spoke out. "One summer, when I was six years old, I fell ill with fainting spells. It was July and very hot but I could not stop shivering. Many people were summoned from every corner of the Peloponnesus but no one could break the spells. The only thing that helped my fever was some snow that several young men brought down in a burlap bag from the crown of Taygetus. It took them a full day to climb there and another day to come back but despite all this attention and concern the spells still lingered. In desperation, my mother hustled me on a donkey and together we traveled all the way into Sparta where an old woman whose name I do not remember took one look at me and exclaimed: 'Someone has cast the evil eye on this child!' My mother became alarmed but the old woman consoled her and said, 'Do not be afraid, my secret prescription will cure him.'"

"What secret prescription?" asked Jason.

Orestes' fingers went to the amulet that hung from his neck. "Man can accomplish many things but he can never defeat the curse of the eye without the secret prescription . . ."

Pappa Sotiri grabbed him by the arm. "In the name of the Father, what is this prescription? Speak!"

"It is a series of mystical words."

"What are these words? Tell us!" cried the priest.

"I am forbidden."

"Who forbids you?" said Pappa Sotiri, flashing his gold cross in front of Orestes' face. "Evil has no power over this. If you know what the secret prescription is, then reveal it. You have my solemn promise that no harm shall befall you."

Jason laughed. "I cannot understand all this anxiety over something so ridiculous."

The priest was obsessed. "In God's name, must I squeeze it out of you, Orestes?"

"It comes from a parable . . ."

"Go on."

". . . Christ was walking with His Mother along the shore of the Dead Sea one day and they got hungry. She spread out

100

a golden cloth over the sand and they sat to eat. After the meal Christ noticed that several crumbs of bread had fallen on the cloth so He folded it together then shook it over the sea. The water immediately became troubled and great waves began lashing the shore . . ."

"Continue."

Orestes again displayed the amulet. "Do you know what is inside this?"

Jason spoke to his glass of ouzo. "The same crumbs that Christ shook over the Dead Sea."

"Not all the crumbs," stammered Orestes.

"Where are the rest?" sneered Barba Manolis.

"The patriarch and the pope have them!" shouted Pavlo with disgust. "Friends of Greece, what has happened to us? In the name of Zeus, I am getting tired of all these myths and fairy tales . . . Pandora boxes, Medusa hairs, Gordian knots, and now bread crumbs!"

"You started it," retorted Barba Manolis. "You and your evil eye."

Jason pulled Kostaki out of his chair and led him to the rear of the taverna. Kostaki tried to go back to the discussion but Jason pushed him into a chair and held him there.

"What do you want?" said Kostaki.

"I want to know why you came back to Livani."

"Christ and the Virgin, I already explained!"

"Explained what?"

"I said I will tell you some other time."

"I want to know now," Jason persisted. "Your mother and father are both dead. Your sister is married and living in Sparta. You have no one here, absolutely no one. And yet you came back to this goddamn village. Why?"

"I do not want to talk about it, Jason."

"Damn it, you were in Athens. Do you realize that? You left this shitty little village to go to Athens. And now you are back."

Kostaki squirmed in the chair.

"You make me sick," said Jason.

"Athens is not what you think," Kostaki retaliated. "It was exciting when we were in the Reserves but we were just passing through. Athens is not the same today. The place is noisy and dirty. The only thing on everyone's mind is *money!* I had to work my ass off, and for what? Just to get by, just to pay the rent and buy a few groceries. I had no friends. No one cared for me, even if I lay sick and dying."

Jason kicked the leg of the table. "So you came back here to die. Is that it?"

"I will find something to do."

"What?"

"Something. People know me here. In Athens I was a stranger. Everyone is a stranger."

"Do you understand what you have done? Do you really understand? You had a chance, an opportunity to escape and become free, but instead you came crawling back to this prison!"

"Livani is not a prison."

Jason slumped into a chair and poured more ouzo into his glass. Kostaki's hand shook when he lit a cigarette. "I want to get out of here," he said.

"You can go to hell."

"No, I am going to visit the widow Marigo."

Jason was disgusted with him.

"I will wait outside. You can be first."

"She is old enough to be your mother," said Jason.

"So what? Are you coming?"

Jason did not bother to answer him.

Kostaki went as far as the nearest table. With the cigarette still dangling from the side of his mouth, he took a long drink from a wine bottle then held it high after it was drained. "This is the way we drink in Athens!" He reached for another bottle and repeated it for the benefit of Yeros Panayiotis.

Pappa Sotiri bade everyone good night and hobbled out of

the taverna. Eyes flashing with mischief, Pavlo waited until the priest closed the door. "Friends of the Symposium, there was a priest in a small village near Sparta who owned seven hundred olive trees but like everything that a priest possesses they were sadly neglected. One day he put on his best robes, trimmed his beard, and climbed to the tower of his church. When the people of the village heard the bell they flocked to the church, crying, 'Who died, Pappa? Who died?' He calmed everyone down and said, 'My children, the Virgin tapped me on the head last night and awoke me from a deep sleep. "Go sound your bell," she said. "Tell your people that I have buried my miraculous icon somewhere in your olive groves. As soon as it is found all the people in your village will be cured of their infirmities!"' Even while he was talking, they all rushed out of the church, grabbed their picks and shovels, and swarmed into the priest's olive groves. They did not stop digging until nightfall. For the first time in years those poor trees stretched their roots in gratitude. The priest waited until everyone had gone home and then he sneaked into his church. Finding an old icon in the dirty cellar, he wiped it clean and quickly buried it in a place where he was certain everyone would dig the next day. A small child found it and the whole village lost its mind. Armies of priests and monks converged upon the olive groves. They examined the icon and proclaimed it a miracle worker. What else could they do? Friends of Greece, that village drowned itself in liturgies. The festivities lasted a whole month, and when the dust finally settled, the icon was carried into the church and mounted on a marble pedestal. And there it stands to this very day. If you should ever visit that village, you will see not only the miraculous icon but the richest, most cultivated olive groves in the Peloponnesus. Ne, ti, ri, rem!"

It was well past midnight. Kostaki began performing again, picking up a full glass of wine with his teeth and drinking from it without using his hands. Jason could not bear the sight of him. Gulping down the last of the ouzo, he pushed back his chair and walked out of the taverna. Pavlo caught up to him in the street. He tried to keep pace with Jason but after they passed the square he stopped. Legs tottering, he braced himself against the marble horse of Kolokotronis then opened the fly of his trousers. Jason kept walking. Before he reached the opposite side of the street, Pavlo's voice swooned into his ears: "Flow gently, friend wine. Flow gently from my barrel. There now, go off somewhere and sleep. We shall meet again tomorrow." Suddenly he started running toward Jason, his fly still unbuttoned. "You see, friend Jason," he cried, "Athens is not the answer. Look what happened to your friend Kostaki. He came crawling back here, a nobody. I tell you, there is only one solution, one cure: *America!*"

3

Another month unpeeled itself, October throwing its cold breath over Livani, Jason burying himself in the taverna every night, wine and cigarettes, Pavlo's persistent reminders about America, Kostaki's horny remarks, the endless struggle in his brain between Danae and the quest for peace, not knowing where to find it or even how to begin. And in the end, his mother's dour face. The stale repetition of mirth and guilt, wanting one thing and doing the other, hating himself then starting all over again.

The work in the groves was finished. All these weeks he had avoided Danae, knowing that if he got too close to her he would want to touch her, kiss her; drive himself into a deeper pit of frustration and despair. He did see her a few times during September but the meetings were casual, mostly in broad daylight—either on the square or outside her father's shop. Her mother's condition had improved and she was now taking short strolls with Danae around the village.

On the feast day of Saint Demetrios he saw Danae coming down the steps of the church. She was alone. He waited until she crossed the street before drawing close to her. "Danae, I must speak to you," he said.

She looked pale and troubled.

"Danae, I have been going crazy these past weeks, not seeing you, not holding you in my arms . . ."

"What do you want, Jason?"

"I am trying to tell you how much I have missed you, how much I have needed you."

Her eyes were cold, unreceptive.

"Danae, I am speaking to you."

"Please move away. I have to go home."

"How is your mother?"

"The same."

"I saw you walking with her yesterday."

"I know."

"Is this all you can say?"

She tried to move around him but he blocked her path.

"Jason, I am not in the mood for games."

"Have you heard from the University?"

"Yes."

"What did they say?"

"I excelled in all the examinations."

"Then you are accepted?"

"In a way."

"I do not follow you."

"The University is holding back all scholarship funds."

"For what reason?"

"The government needs the money for military purposes, to strengthen our country's defenses."

"But what about your scholarship?"

"It will have to wait until the funds are released. Jason, I cannot linger here. I am expected at home."

He took hold of her hand but she pulled it away. Her eyes were flashing with anger. "Why are you still in Livani?" she exclaimed. "You said you were going to leave for Athens in the fall and you are still here!"

He stepped back and did not say another word.

The next morning he stationed himself in the square, his eyes fixed on her front door. She did not come out until midday. He waited until she walked past her father's shop before he caught up to her. Her face still had that troubled look.

"Danae, please do not walk away from me. I must talk to you."

She stopped and, with her head down, started to weep. He took her into his arms and kissed her wet cheek. "Danae, I wish you would tell me what is wrong."

"My mother is going to die!"

"But I thought there was nothing wrong with her."

"That is what I thought also, but last night my father told me the truth . . ."

"What truth?"

"She has a fatal blood disease. The specialist in Athens discovered it."

"And she never told you about it?"

"She told only my father."

"But why did she keep it from you?"

"So that I would not worry about her. She wanted me to do well in the examinations for the University." Danae broke into sobs. "Jason, I was so wrong about her. I thought she was selfish and wanted to keep me under her eyes for the rest of my life but instead she hid her grief and her pain . . ."

He kissed her again on the cheek. "Did the specialist say how long she has?"

"It is but a matter of time. My father was never going to tell me but yesterday afternoon I saw Kyra Maria give my mother an injection and I realized that there was something seriously wrong with her. I spoke to my father and he finally revealed the truth."

"The specialist could be wrong."

"No," she cried.

"Perhaps it is only neurasthenia. She has never been a strong woman."

"No, Jason. The specialist submitted her to many tests. He also got the opinion of another specialist." She broke into sobs once again. "I feel so terrible, Jason. My mother is going to die!"

He tried to whisper words of courage to her but she kept sobbing and trembling in his arms. He realized now how hopeless it had been, not seeing her in weeks, avoiding her when his heart ached for her.

The sky was infested with black clouds. It started to rain. He took off his jacket and threw it over her head. "Will I see you tonight, Jason?" she asked.

"Yes."

"I need you very much."

"I love you, Danae. I love you with all my heart."

"What about Athens?"

"Athens will have to wait. I could never leave you now."

"But I do not want you to stay here on my account. I know how much your heart has been set on leaving."

"It is not important now," said Jason. "We can talk about it some other time."

•   •

As soon as he walked into the taverna that afternoon Kostaki came rushing toward him, swept him into his slender arms, kissed him on both cheeks and treated him to a glass of ouzo. Jason ordered another ouzo and soon the taverna began filling with faces. Master Theophilos approached their table, waving a newspaper in front of Jason. "Things look very bleak, my son. Look at this map. We have the Italians on our left hand and the Germans on our right."

"Do not forget the Turks," shouted Pavlo from the next table. "They have been sitting on our heads since the fall of Byzantium!"

Yeros Panayiotis started weeping. Kostaki went to console him but Pavlo pulled him away. "The old frog cries every time he hears the word 'Turk.' Get away from him. He is acting."

Master Theophilos turned and addressed himself to everyone in the taverna. "I wish you would all be serious for a change. We are living in critical times."

"That is true, friend teacher, but let us not forget that time also pulls us into joyful moments. Nothing is permanent. We have war one moment, peace the next. This is the law of human existence. In the name of Heraclitus, life constantly changes."

"The philosopher!" jeered Barba Manolis.

"I sleep with your coffee grounds!"

"And I sleep with your lunatic ancestors," retorted the tavern-keeper.

Jason asked them to be quiet. "I think we should pay heed to Master Theophilos. If we are invaded how will we defend ourselves? We have a few dozen ancient tanks, no antitank guns, and less than a hundred antiaircraft guns to protect the entire country. Our army has the grand total of seventy-five thousand men."

"What about the Reserves?" said Kostaki, inflating his chest.

"You know as well as I that the Reserves are ill-equipped, poorly trained, and definitely no match for Mussolini's superior forces. He has eight divisions massed on the Albanian border, each reinforced with artillery and assault tanks. One of these divisions has over three thousand mules and donkeys to carry supplies and ammunition over the mountain passes. Mussolini has an excellent navy. His air force is modern and powerful, with bases in Brindisi and many parts of Albania."

A long silence fell on the taverna.

"And now let us consider *our* navy," Jason continued. "We have one very old armored cruiser, twenty torpedo boats, a half-dozen destroyers, six submarines, and two mine sweepers. As for our air force, we have exactly one hundred and fifty-one planes."

Yeros Panayiotis rose to his feet. "I predict that if war is declared, Greece will be crushed within twenty-four hours!"

"Friend of the cane, you forget one very important item which is the source of our greatest strength," snapped Pavlo.

"And what is that?"

"Our spirit, our fighting Greek spirit. It is true that during times of peace we Greeks are always clashing with each other, as we do here in this taverna, but when war comes we forget our petty arguments and join hands against the enemy. This was true in ancient times and it is true today."

"I am afraid it will take more than spirit to defeat Mussolini," said Jason.

"You are entitled to your opinion, friend nephew, and I am entitled to mine. History will prove who is right."

Jason ordered a bottle of wine for the table. From the far corner of the taverna several men issued loud cries of support for Prime Minister Metaxas. Toasts were raised.

"Listen to the fools," said Pavlo, helping himself to more wine. "They are cheering for a dictator. They do not understand that the rotten fish always begins to smell from the head. Praise Zeus, I will soon be liberated from all this nonsense. Yes, friends of the new world, I am about to make final arrangements for my departure to America. I have prepared myself by studying the language. I know everything there is to know about customs and manners. Ah, how my soul thirsts for that first glimpse of the Statue of Liberty! How do you do, friend madam? I am pleased to make your acquaintance. The first president of the United States of America was George Washington, the father of our country. I pledge allegiance to the flag . . ."

Jason was the only one in the taverna who did not laugh. He lit a cigarette then handed the pack to Kostaki. By this time, Pavlo was possessed. "You are surprised to hear me speak the language of America? Friends of liberty, I have worked hard, studying, preparing myself for that glorious day when I will look Metaxas in the eye and say: 'Friend Dictator, I cannot breathe in this country any longer. I am going to a place where the right hand does not know the left. And to you, friend Paul, spineless figurehead of a king, I say farewell also. In the name of Abraham Lincoln, I am an American citizen. I live in New York and I own three restaurants. I have money in two banks. I drive a Cadillac automobile. I voted for Franklin Delano Roosevelt and his wife Eleanor. America, I love you!' "

•   •

On their way home Pavlo pulled up next to the plane tree in the square and grabbed Jason by the arm. His voice had ground itself into a coarse whisper. "Friend Jason, we cannot wait any longer."

"What do you mean?"

"We must do it right away, immediately!"

"Do what?"

"Go to America."

"You are drunk," said Jason.

"No, I am sober, very sober."

"You will feel better in the morning."

Pavlo tightened the grip on his arm. "We must go now. Put your trust in me, friend Jason. You will never regret it. This is our last chance. We must stop talking about it and act. Do you want to rot in this village, manacled to your father's olive trees, strapped to that nereid, chained forever to this barren land? America is waiting for us!"

Jason glared at him. "What about your wife, little Renio?"

"I will send for them as soon as we get settled. Your mother and father will come too. We will all live in America with dignity. Come."

"Now, this very moment?"

Pavlo shook his head with impatience. "Tomorrow is Sunday. We will leave the next day. No explanations, no good-byes, no tears and gnashing of teeth. I have planned this day for a long time, friend Jason. It must be done exactly as I say."

"And what are we going to use for money?"

Pavlo responded in a harsh shrill. "You must not breathe a word of this, do you hear? My brother Stathis sent me money a long time ago. I have kept it hidden in a safe place, just for this purpose."

"Aunt Yianoula does not know?"

"Of course not."

Jason pulled away from him. "I have to think about this."

"No, you will think about the nereid and you will run into her arms. She will never let you go!"

"But you are asking me to forget about Athens . . ."

"Yes."

". . . turn my back on my mother and father."

"It will only be for a short while. Once we get settled they will join us."

"It is not right," said Jason, his voice weakening. Pavlo was relentless. "Friend Jason, I cannot do it by myself. I need you. Do you understand? If we go together everyone will be proud of us—but if I go by myself they will curse me and say I abandoned them. I will never be able to live it down. This is my last opportunity, yours also. We must do it now, otherwise we both shall die!"

Jason thought about the thick loneliness of the night, the desolate square, the narrow streets leading nowhere, the eternal confinement of the olive groves. He thought about Danae.

Would he still feel the same way toward her after their first child, the second and third? Would she feel the same way about him? *Jason, the fat father, wallowing in his olive groves, drinking in the taverna every night, cursing his fate—wishing, always wishing he had gone to America.*

"I will come with you," he said.

"You are not joking, friend Jason?"

"No."

Pavlo started weeping with joy. "I will never forget this. You have made me the happiest man on earth."

"How are we going to do it?" said Jason.

"I will meet you here in the square, early Monday morning. We will walk to the railroad station in Kalamata . . ."

"Walk?"

"Do you want a full dress parade?" Pavlo winced. "We will walk casually as though we have no place in mind. These hills have eyes, friend Jason. No one must know what we are going to do. After we reach Kalamata, we will walk leisurely around the main streets, visiting one shop after another. We will have a quiet meal somewhere and then, making certain that no one is watching us, we will sneak off to the railroad station, buy our tickets to Athens, and the next day we will be on board a ship at Piraeus, bound for America!"

Jason became silent.

"I want you to promise me one thing, friend Jason."

"What?"

"You must never see the nereid again."

"Why?"

"She will twist your mind and beg you not to leave."

"I have already decided," said Jason.

"Nevertheless, I want you to promise me."

"I promise."

●   ●

He was back in the taverna the next night, talking with Pavlo, still wondering how he could go through with it, washing his hands of Livani forever, never seeing Danae again. Pavlo was a new man. He bounced from table to table, treated everyone, and even was kind to Barba Manolis.

A few moments after vespers, Pappa Sotiri walked into the taverna, ordered a medium-sweet coffee then took a table near the window. Pavlo joined him. "Wisdom and fame run in my family, your holiness. My grandfather Elias was the poet laureate of the Peloponnesus, a man who could not read or write, mind you. But twice a month he took the schoolteacher into the mountains with him. They lived in caves, under trees, on cliffs. They ate berries and roots, hunted rabbits, and when they returned from the wilderness Grandfather Elias had a fresh batch of poems under his arm. You ask how? The schoolteacher was his stenographer. Grandfather Elias dictated every word."

The priest had his mind elsewhere.

"I wish you would keep quiet," said Jason from the adjacent table.

"Why?"

"No one is listening to you."

"The walls have ears, friend nephew. Someday I will be remembered."

There was a sharp sound of horse's hoofs in the street and Kostaki went outside to investigate. He returned a few moments later, followed by a man in an officer's uniform. "My name is Captain Drakos," he said, clicking his heels before stooping to kiss the priest's hand.

"What brings you to our village at this time of night?" asked Pappa Sotiri.

The captain shot a quick glance around the taverna. "Are you not aware of what has happened?"

Pavlo took the floor. "Here in this remote village, friend captain, we are aware only of God and Taygetus. Your name tells me that you are from Sparta. How are things in the ancient city?"

"We are at war!"

"Are you squabbling with the Athenians again?"

Captain Drakos pulled off his coat. "This very hour Mussolini's armies are invading northern Greece. There is heavy fighting in the mountains of Epirus."

"You see, my children, I was right," declared Master Theophilos.

The priest crossed himself and started murmuring a prayer but Pavlo stopped him. "This is no time for the miroloy. Friend captain, when did all this happen?"

"Early yesterday morning, the twenty-eighth of October. Mussolini's ambassador to Greece issued this ultimatum to Metaxas: 'Greeks, sit on your hands while I pass through your country.' In God's name, Metaxas gave him Greece's answer: '*No!*'"

"Bravo for the prime minister!" shouted Barba Manolis. He offered a glass of ouzo to the captain.

"My horse is outside. He is hungry and soaked with sweat," said Captain Drakos.

Pappa Sotiri cleared his throat. "Barba Costa will attend to him. He keeps a clean stable. You there, Anastasi, bring the captain's horse to Barba Costa. What else can we do for you, captain? Surely you must be hungry?"

Captain Drakos nodded his head stiffly. Everything about him was stiff and precise. "First, you must sound your bell. Summon everyone to the church."

"Tonight?"

"Right now."

The priest stood up. He seemed confused with the quick turn of events. His steps were unsteady. Kostaki put out his cigarette and exclaimed, "I will sound the bell, your holiness."

"Good," said Pappa Sotiri.

Captain Drakos accepted another glass of ouzo from Barba Manolis. The tavern-keeper hurried into the back room and came back with a plate of cheese, olives, and bread. Between mouthfuls, the captain announced, "I want every male between the ages of seventeen and seventy at the church as soon as possible, especially those in the Reserves."

Pappa Sotiri led the way out of the taverna. The night was cold. The houses lay in darkness. The first peal of the bell split the sky wide open, sending its sharp echo against the chest of Taygetus. Dogs began howling. Soon a wave of people gushed into the square.

Jason waited until Kostaki came down from the tower and together they walked into the church. Pappa Sotiri slid open the door of the iconostasis and slowly climbed to the ambo. A hush fell over the church.

"Good souls of Livani, Greece has been invaded by the Fascist armies of Mussolini. Our beloved country is at war . . ."

"Christ and the Virgin!" moaned an old woman.

Another woman fell to her knees before the icon of Saint Chrysostomos and began crossing herself. A young boy fainted. The priest lifted his hands and tried to calm everyone but panic had already swept through the church. Men and women jostled each other, rushing frantically for the door. Both Jason and Kostaki tried to hold them back but no one listened. Suddenly Pappa Sotiri began chanting:

> *Invincible Commander*
> *And Glorious Liberator,*
> *Save us from this danger*
> *So that we can again cry unto Thee:*
> *"Hail, Thou full of grace!"*

His words were a balm for their terror. The stampede stopped immediately and everyone filed back into the church. In a trembling voice, Pappa Sotiri embraced them all.

> *I know you*
> *From the fearful cut*
> *Of your sword.*

I know you
From your eye,
Which with one glance,
Measures the earth . . .

Jason had not sung the anthem since his childhood but, like everyone else in the church, he followed the priest's lips. When Pappa Sotiri repeated it, Jason caught a glimpse of Danae standing at the opposite side of the church, her gaze fastened on the icon of the Virgin.

•   •

Pavlo was waiting for him on the stairs of the church, his face blotched with anxiety. "The square at daybreak tomorrow," he rasped.

"What?" said Jason.

"Have you been speaking to that nereid? Did she twist your mind?"

"What are you talking about?"

"America! We have to leave tomorrow morning . . ."

"But everything has changed. It is impossible now."

"There, you see. She did twist your mind!"

"You were in that church," said Jason. "You heard every word. We are at war with the Italians."

"That has nothing to do with us. If we leave right away no one will notice it. A casual stroll into Kalamata . . ."

"I never expected this from you," said Jason.

"What?"

"You want us to run away, like cowards."

"Cowards live, friend Jason. Heroes die!"

"Have you forgotten your own words?"

"What words?"

"Saturday night at the taverna, you said our fighting Greek spirit was our greatest source of strength, and when war comes we all join hands against the enemy."

Pavlo fell silent.

"This is exactly what you said."

"Friend Jason, think carefully. You are in the Reserves. You will be the first to be drafted."

"I know."

"Then stop being a fool. A leisurely walk to Kalamata, the train to Athens, the ship, and we will be on our way."

"How can you leave Greece when she needs you most?" Jason exclaimed.

"Who is Greece? Does she care about me? Did she ever care about me?"

Jason started to pull away from him.

"Then you are not coming?" Pavlo shouted.

"No."

"You will be sorry, friend Jason. All your life you will regret it. Pay heed to my words. This opportunity will never come to you again!"

Jason swung into the street.

"It is that nereid," cried Pavlo, seizing him by the arm. "I told you not to think about her. I warned you!"

Jason tugged his arm free and walked away. But before he could cross the street, Pavlo's snarling wrath fell on his back: "Goodbye, friend Jason. Stay here and die with your olive trees, with your nereid and your foolish patriotism. I am going to America!"

4

His father came with him the next morning. A long table was set up under the narthex of the church and Captain Drakos was busily filling out papers. A line of men stretched from the church to the street: wiry shepherds, dark-skinned fishermen, salt-gatherers from the Tigani peninsula.

Kostaki was the first to be conscripted.

"State your name and age," said Captain Drakos.

"Kostaki Angelakos. I am twenty-two."

"You are in the Reserves?"

"Yes."

"Where did you train?"

"In Macedonia."

"What is your unit?"

"The Spartan Battalion."

"You will join it at the railroad station in Kalamata on five November, nine o'clock in the morning. Is that clear?"

"Yes, captain."

"Be in full uniform."

"Yes, captain."

Jason was next. After him came Kitso, the son of Barba Manolis. He was twenty-four and the father of two small children. He seldom visited the taverna. Barba Manolis stood erect and proud when Captain Drakos wrote Kitso's name down. After he had finished with the Reserves, the captain turned to the others but before he could say a word to them Pavlo appeared from nowhere and exclaimed, "Friend captain, you can sign me up also!"

Jason was stunned.

"How old are you?" asked Captain Drakos.

"Thirty-eight."

"Were you ever in the Reserves?"

"No."

"You must say No, captain."

"No, captain."

"Are you married?"

"Yes, captain. I have one child, a girl named Renio. She is six years old."

Jason was still dazed when Pavlo finally walked away from the table. A young fisherman stepped forward trembling. The fingers of his left hand were missing.

"What happened to your fingers?" asked Captain Drakos.

"A sand shark bit them off when I was twelve."

"Why are you shaking? Do you not want to defend your country?"

The fisherman gave him a sick smile. "How can I shoot a rifle with all these fingers missing?"

"Use your thumb," said Captain Drakos, writing down the man's name. A wave of muffled laughter rolled over the church. Throughout the long procedure Jason's father remained standing near the vestry, not saying a word.

Many were rejected for missing limbs, tubercular coughs, withered arms and legs, strange behavior. The older men huddled around Captain Drakos and listened intently to his instructions about the home guard, sentry duty, calisthenics, and daily marches. Finally Captain Drakos turned and addressed everyone in the church: "Raise your right hands and repeat after me: 'I hereby swear that I will be true to my country and to the King of all Greeks; that I will obey and be loyal to them, subjugate myself to my superiors and carry out willingly any command they give. I swear to defend the flag until the last drop of blood is drained from my body, never to forsake it or be cut off from it, and always to conduct myself as a faithful and trustworthy soldier. So help me God!' "

Jason was entangled in doubt and confusion when he came out of the church. In a few hours Mussolini's faceless hand would be pulling him away from Livani, from his father's olive groves, from Danae . . . dragging him across the Peloponnesus, into Athens. But this was not the way he had wanted to leave.

He barely heard Captain Drakos' final words from the church steps. "The Reserves have until five November to put their affairs in order. At nine o'clock of that morning they will report in full uniform to the railroad station at Kalamata where they will be assigned rifles and ammunition, and then taken by train to Athens." He looked at the priest and asked, "How far is it to Petra?"

"A half-hour."

"Which road?"

"Follow the north route. There, on your right hand."

Barba Costa was waiting for the captain in the street. "I rubbed your horse down, Mister Captain. I also gave him two buckets of oats.

Captain Drakos thanked him.

Pappa Sotiri blessed him after he got on his horse. "Go to the Good, my son. May God protect you. May God protect Greece!"

The captain bolted away in a storm of dust and slowly the men began scattering for their homes. Jason's father had already crossed the square. Jason hurried to catch up with him but he was instantly manacled by Pavlo's booming voice. "Friends of the Royal Greek Army, we shall soon be staring Mussolini in the face!"

"I thought you would be well on your way to America by now," said Jason.

"American has waited all this time for me. She can be patient for a few more months."

"I am sorry . . ."

"About what?"

"For thinking you were a coward," said Jason.

Pavlo embraced him. In a boisterous voice, he yelled at Marko: "Friend of the olive, have you no love for your country? Why did you not step forward to enlist?"

"I am too old," said Marko. "You heard the captain. They do not want anyone over forty-five for active duty."

"In the name of Ares, you should have made some effort. What will everyone in Livani think?"

Marko stopped walking. Flinging an icy stare at Pavlo, he said, "You may have fooled them with your idiotic bravado— but you did not fool me."

"Ne ti, ri, rem . . ."

"You silly bastard!"

"How dare you speak to me in that manner? I am a soldier in the Royal Greek Army. You are nothing but a home guard, parading through the streets of Livani with a broom on your shoulder. Halt, who goes there, friend or foe? What is the password? *'God is Good! God is Good!'* "

Marko pulled away from him in disgust.

When they passed Panos' cobbler shop Pavlo whispered to Jason, "The nereid is sleeping in her grotto, friend Jason. Go wake her up. Give her a final screw before we leave!"

Jason slew him with his eyes.

5

He spent his last hours in Livani with Danae. They clung to each other like wet leaves on a pond. She did not cry but every time he kissed her a distant look swept over her eyes. In a hollow voice, she promised to wait for him. Even after he released her, she did not weep, but when he slowly walked away, she covered her face with both hands. He could not bear her frozen look, her final wave.

He was stifled by the long wagon ride to Kalamata with his mother and father, Pavlo's fear masqueraded in jokes, the thick crowds at the railroad station, the army doctor's questions, the cold stethoscope on his chest, the train pulling away.

Kostaki did not come with them. That same stethoscope detected something in his lungs and he was instantly rejected. Jason tried to console him but the train was calling him for the last time.

Cities and towns skipped by the window of his compartment: Kyparissia, Pyrgos, Amalias, Patras. From the moment they left Kalamata Pavlo stuck close to Jason's side, telling him things he already knew, that his father had been a teacher in Sparta and was a direct descendant of Mavromichalis, the revered name of the Peloponnesus, that one of his ancestors was Bey of Mani, another, the war minister under King Otto, and still another, the chief aide to Kolokotronis at Kalavryta in 1821 when the standard of revolt was raised against the Turks. They went in and out of Corinth and were well on their way to Eleusis, and Pavlo kept rambling on until Jason finally closed his eyes and feigned sleep.

The next afternoon they were walking in the streets of Athens. The city was overflowing with soldiers. The sidewalk cafés that lined Omonoia Square were jammed. Constitution Square was turmoil: long queues stretching along the sidewalks and into the shops, people everywhere. Despite the heavy pall of war, Athens hid her sorrow like a queen. Her stores carried lavish displays in the windows, music poured out of the tavernas, people walked arm-in-arm singing patriotic songs. No matter where Jason looked, the Acropolis loomed above him, proudly watching over the city, the brilliant sun engulfing the marble columns, its light swarming over the pediments.

They entered a small taverna just off Omonoia Square, sat at a table near the window and clapped their hands for a waiter. They both ordered lamb and pilaf. It was the first substantial meal Jason had eaten in three days. Pavlo joked with the waiters as they danced from table to table, shouting their orders to the kitchen.

It was dark when they came outside. The window shades in all the shops were drawn. Pulling up their collars, they ran across the street toward the sound of bouzoukia, the voices of women.

Every table in the taverna was taken. On a small platform sat five musicians. A half-dozen women in long silk dresses stood at the bar. Pavlo drooled when two of them approached. "Buy us a drink?" said one. She was the taller of the two and much older. The other came close to Jason but did not speak.

"How about it, soldiers?" said the seasoned hen. "Buy us a drink."

Pavlo ordered four cognacs. In time they found a table and sat. The younger girl did not lift her eyes from Jason's hands. "Where do you come from?" she asked.

"The Peloponnesus."

"But that is a large place. What is the name of your village?"

"Livani."

She sighed. "It is a pretty name. Please buy me another drink."

"You have not touched the first," said Jason.

"I like to arrange them in a straight line."

Pavlo was fondling the older woman's knee. "Do you want to dance a Sirto with me?" he asked.

She shook her head.

"Why not?"

"We are not permitted because of the war."

"Then what are you doing here?"

"We talk to the soldiers; help them forget."

Pavlo hurled a starved look toward Jason. "I will meet you at the foot of the Acropolis in two hours."

"Where are you going?"

Pavlo had his eyes riveted to the older woman's legs. "Friend Jason, this is no time for questions."

"But what about Aunt Yianoula and little Renio?" whispered Jason.

Pavlo did not bother to answer. He grabbed the woman by the arm and walked out of the taverna with her.

The younger girl was running her fingers over both glasses. "I would like to make you happy," she murmured.

"When?" asked Jason.

"Right now. My apartment is not far from here."

"What about the cognacs?"

"Leave them on the table."

He finished his cognac and waited while she went after her coat. A light rain was falling when they came into the street. She linked her arm to his and led him across the dimly lit square, past a marble statesman standing poised on a small plot of grass. They entered a street tight with houses; an old taxi whirled by, splattering them with mud and water. After a few blocks, she stopped in front of an arched doorway and dug into her bag for some keys. There were two rooms in the apartment—a tiny kitchen and a wide living room with a brown divan. A neatly embroidered cloth was draped over the table in the kitchen. Directly above the divan rested a tiny icon shelf. A holy light still sputtered inside the rose-colored glass.

"I have some ouzo," she said, taking off her coat and placing it over the divan. She brought him a glass and filled it with ouzo.

"What is your name?" he asked.

"Nikkie. What is yours?"

"Jason."

She hung her coat in the closet and asked him to sit on the divan.

"Do you live here alone?" he asked.

"Yes. Elena made all the arrangements."

"Who is Elena?"

"The woman who went off with your friend."

"Where is your home?"

She did not reply.

He smiled at her. "What is the name of your village?"

"Kasteli. It is a small town near Larissa. How I hated that place! My father died when I was twelve. Every day I begged my mother to leave and move to Salonika but she would not hear of it. When I became seventeen I crept out of the house one day and walked all the way to Larissa. I slept in the railroad station that night and the next morning I was on the train to Athens."

"You ran away?"

"Yes."

"How long ago was that?"

"Last year."

"Then you are eighteen?"

"Yes."

He took a sip of ouzo from his glass.

"I know what you are thinking," she murmured, her eyes moistening. "But I will not stay at that taverna forever. As soon as I raise enough money I will . . ."

She broke into sobs.

He gave her the ouzo and implored her to drink some of it. She tried. "It is not true what I said about Kasteli. I do not hate it. It is Athens that I hate—the crowds, the noise, the unclean smells. You would adore Kasteli. It is so peaceful and quiet."

"Do you intend to go back?"

She nodded. "After my mother dies."

"I do not understand."

"I must wait until then. If I go back now she would never accept me."

"Because you ran away?"

"Yes. I disgraced her."

She tried another sip of ouzo. He waited a moment then took the glass away and embraced her. He put his lips to her neck and heard her gasp. He had difficulty unclasping her dress. She threw her hands behind her back and helped him. The sight of her breasts scorched his brain.

"You will be gentle with me," she whispered.

He shuddered from the violent explosion in his ears. Clearly, he saw the mountains of Macedonia, the snow, the cannons and blood. In a few hours he would be staring Charon in the face, but now this fleeting moment was upon him, soft, warm, beckoning. *Why are you waiting, foolish Jason? Now!*

FOUR

Without reason or explanation, the train was delayed in Athens for ten days. Disorder and confusion, hundreds of cots crammed on the dirty floor of the railroad station, officers barking at soldiers, threats and promises in the same breath. Greek bedlam.

Every night after dinner, Pavlo begged Jason to go to the taverna with him but Jason refused. It rained almost daily. On the first clear day Jason kept Pavlo waiting while he climbed the Propylaia steps to the Parthenon. He sat on a marble slab and picked up a small stone. *Yes, my little Icarus, I held God in my hands that day . . .*

Tenderly he placed the stone back on the exact spot and stood up. Danae kept infiltrating his brain. He did not want to think about her, about his parents, about anyone or anything in Livani.

Pavlo was pacing back and forth on the street when he came down from the Parthenon. "What the hell were you doing up there all this time?" he exclaimed.

"I wanted to see something," said Jason.

"In the name of Pericles, what was the great attraction? There is nothing remaining up there but broken chunks of marble. For the last time, are you coming with me to the taverna?"

"No."

"But I learned that we are leaving tomorrow morning. We will not see another woman in months."

"Good," said Jason.

"The young one keeps asking for you."

"She should go back to her village."

Pavlo decided not to leave the railroad station that night. Mumbling and cursing, he flung himself on his cot and even refused to talk. Jason went to a small restaurant a few blocks away and brought back some roast lamb, bread and cheese, a bottle of retsina wine, but Pavlo remained sullen and shoved everything away. At nine the next morning, the train—driven by two powerful engines—pulled slowly out of the station. The soldiers had to work until the last moment, packing all the freight cars with food and equipment. Within an hour, the train left Athens far behind, rumbling past weird patterns of shadows and sunlight, outracing the Aegean, picking up its own reflection and splattering it over the wrinkled face of the sea. The hours lost themselves under the steady drone of the iron wheels. In the middle of the afternoon they came upon the first plains of Thessaly. Great pastures rolled into view, a fleeting farmhouse, a sparkling white church, women working in the fields. Greece unwinding herself before Jason's eyes. Pavlo was not interested. He kept his eyes away from the window, fidgeting with his hands, staring at the other soldiers in the compartment, not saying a word.

"At times, I wish we were not related," said Jason.

Pavlo glared at him.

"I cannot understand your behavior. From the moment we left Livani you have turned into a different person, forgetting your family, thinking only of prostitutes . . ."

Pavlo left his seat and opened the door of the compartment. He stood in the passageway for a long time and then came back and sat down. He closed his eyes. Several hours later, there was a grinding sound of brakes, a piercing shrill. A long ramp came into view, a railroad station. *Larissa.*

•   •

One of the engines needed repairs and they had to remain in Larissa for three days. Pavlo was disappointed. This was not

Athens. There were shops and restaurants here, but no tavernas with women. In the mornings, the young girls came out to shop but they were always accompanied by their mothers, who gripped them firmly by the hand. Pavlo had no desire to explore the city. Jason tried to persuade him several times but eventually gave up. Each of the three mornings he left the train early and walked around the city by himself, dissecting every corner, discovering quaint little streets and houses. Larissa lay on the right bank of a river. Farms and fertile valleys were spread out in endless carpets. He envisioned Nikkie escaping over these same hills, her auburn hair whipped back by the Thessalonian wind.

He thought about Danae.

On the fourth morning the train finally pushed forward again, following a long river that ran parallel with a winding road. Flashes of fire from the straining engines left their imprint on the water. Nameless towns and hamlets danced by the window. Just before sunset they entered into a fortress of mountains. The tired engines groaned and puffed, filling the sky with dense clouds of smoke.

Pavlo spoke for the first time since they left Larissa. "What are those mountains?"

"Olympus," said Jason.

"We must be near Salonika."

"Yes, we should be there tomorrow."

"Are you sure?"

"We might stay over for a few days," said Jason.

"How do you know?"

"One of the soldiers in the next compartment told me," said Jason. "He has an uncle who lives in this area."

Pavlo ate with appetite that night as the train streaked past a necklace of villages. Greece on their left hand, the Aegean on their right. Some of the soldiers in the next compartment started singing guerrilla songs, and almost as though it were yesterday, Jason was following his grandfather down from the hills with the thirty-seven musicians. At the north pass, just before entering Livani, the old man's voice resounded in his heart:

> *Forty guerrillas from Livadia*
> *Where are you going, lads,*
> *Where?*
> *To free Tripoli,*
> *Tripolitsa,*
> *From Turkish hands*
> *And Ali Pasha!*

•   •

They never reached Salonika. Swerving sharply to the left at Platy, the train sped toward Veria, which lay just to the south of Edessa. It happened during the night. Pavlo was heartbroken. He refused to touch a morsel of food even after they stopped at Veria for a few hours. But halfway toward Edessa his face lit up when one of the older soldiers assured him they would stop over at Florina for at least three days. *Florina of the brothels.* Jason remembered the long lines of soldiers waiting their turn in the street, the fair-headed Macedonian women, the old brass beds, the burning taste of raki.

After a few hours a broad plain unfolded, sliced in the center by a wide river, which they followed all the way into Amyntaion. Now Vevi. At midafternoon they were in the heart of Florina.

2

A city of flowers, green with cypresses, streets pulsating from Alexander's footsteps, women attired in bright native costumes and brilliant bonnets. On a plateau below the city, the men of Florina had once battled the mighty Persians and had thrown down their arms, but the women refused to accept defeat. Fighting heroically, they vanquished the enemy, and when Alexander heard of their prowess he decreed that they, and not the men, should wear the honored helmets of heroes. After twenty-five hundred years the women of Florina still wore their ancient bonnets with pride.

Jason had worshipped Alexander throughout his childhood; followed every inch of his journeys across Greece, Egypt, Persia, India; fought beside him at Issus and at Arbela; died with him in Babylonia. And now he was once again in Macedonia, breathing Alexander's air, climbing the high hills that encircled Florina on all sides, spending a whole afternoon at the monastery of Saint Marko, where he lit a candle for his father. Somehow it was not difficult to express his love from a distance even though he could not understand what compelled him, an insignificant flame spiraling into God's eye, seeking special favor and absolution from uncommitted sins.

The zoo was near the railroad station. He visited it with Pavlo one morning. They teased the lions and jackals, fed the tropical birds, stood away from the savage apes. Later in the evening they dined in a small but clean taverna on the street of Alexander the Great: meatballs wrapped in grape leaves, exquisite wine from Amyntaion. They drank until the early hours of morning. There were no young girls sitting at the bar, only mature women with hospitable bosoms. Like the widow Marigo, they never asked questions. In and out quickly, and it was over. War games.

They moved out of Florina on a cold rainy morning. Hardly anyone in the compartment spoke as they crossed the border into Jugoslavia. There were no guerrilla songs, only the steady clang of iron wheels over the tracks. Within an hour they were surrounded by the thousand minarets of Monastir.

The railroad station was chaos, officers yelling at soldiers, commanding them to line up before the waiting lorries. He and Pavlo were assigned to a grizzly sergeant named Michalis. Two hours passed before their lorry finally left the railroad station. Even with their heavy coats, they shivered. The wooden seats were coated with ice. Heavy artillery fire resounded from the west as they rolled across the phlegmatic face of Jugoslavia. Everyone's mouth was taut. Fear poured out of nostrils.

Jason looked back and saw the long row of lorries trailing behind. Eighty-seven. He had counted them at the railroad station before they left. Sergeant Michalis said they were heading directly for the Albanian front and he tried to buoy up their spirits by telling them the British had come to their aid, sending fighter planes and bombers in daily attacks against the Italian positions.

The lorries stopped shortly after midnight on the perimeter of a dense forest. Tents were put up; fires lit. It was too cold to sit and eat. Pavlo hardly touched the lamb stew. Even though he stood close to the fire, covered by a blanket, Jason could not keep warm. The bitter Macedonian wind threatened to blow the tents away. It was impossible to sleep.

After munching on some hard bread and cheese, they set off early the next morning, moving westward across the bleak land, under a moody sky. An hour later, Sergeant Michalis announced, "We should be in Koritsa soon."

"Where is that?" asked Pavlo.

"Albania."

"Are the Italians there?"

Sergeant Michalis measured him. "You are a skinny bastard. What holds you together?"

Pavlo clamped both hands over his crotch. "This!"

A few of the soldiers laughed but Jason felt uncomfortable. He wished that Pavlo would keep his mouth shut. The silly blundering fool, thirty-eight years old and still acting like a child.

The lorries were ravaging the Jugoslavian landscape, leaving the east far behind. The cold was unbearable. Pavlo looked pale; his lips and hands were trembling.

"You should try to eat some bread and cheese," said Jason.

"I am not hungry."

"Force yourself."

"Is there any wine on this lorry?"

"Of course not."

"I hate to admit this, friend Jason, but I wish I were back in Livani."

Jason put some cheese in front of Pavlo's mouth, made him take a bite. He handed him a chunk of bread.

"Friend Jason, I hope they do not separate us. I hope we stay close together."

They were high in the mountains now. Massive peaks loomed on the horizon. They thrashed their arms and stamped their feet in an attempt to get warm. In the middle of the night the lorries finally stopped rolling and they set up camp on the shore of a large lake called Prespa. Bean soup. Again Pavlo ate very little. No one could sleep. Sergeant Michalis returned from a briefing with a group of officers and assembled his unit around one of the fires. "The Italians are boasting to the world that they are going to crush us," he said in a hard voice. "They have even disclosed their plan of attack. It provides for one thrust along the Adriatic coast and another at the far end of the eastern front toward Salonika. Both of these assaults have already been launched but our high command suspects that they are diversionary thrusts. We now feel certain that the main attack has started in the center, at Kalpaki Pass, just north of Ioannina. Intelligence reports tell us that the Italians have tried to cut through the Pindus mountains, hoping to capture the important town of Metsovon."

"The Italians have openly bragged about this plan?" asked Jason.

"Yes."

Pavlo scratched his head. "Are they that stupid?"

"This is what they want us to believe," said Sergeant Michalis.

"How long have you been in the regular army, friend sergeant?"

"Seventeen years."

"When do you intend to retire?"

"After we lick Mussolini."

"Where do you suppose he is?" asked Pavlo.

"Who?"

"Mussolini."

"In Rome, protecting his bald head," grinned one of the soldiers.

Jason was anxious to hear more about the Italian plan of attack. "Sergeant, what happened at Salonika?"

"Because of the hilly terrain," Sergeant Michalis continued, "the Italians got bogged down. But on the Adriatic coast they were very successful because they met hardly any resistance. The best we could throw at them was a brief volley of artillery and some negligible rifle fire from the rural police of that area."

"That is a hell of a way to fight a war," grunted Pavlo.

"It was all a diversion," said Sergeant Michalis.

"Ah, so the Greeks too have a plan?"

"Of course. Papagos is one step ahead of Mussolini."

"Who is Papagos, friend sergeant?"

"You are a dumb bastard," barked Sergeant Michalis. "General Papagos is our Commanding Officer. He is the brains behind the Royal Greek Army."

Pavlo huffed. "Exactly. He is right *behind* us, a real general!"

Sergeant Michalis angrily shook his head. "You cannot say that about General Papagos. In a few days you will see for yourself. He is always in the front lines, a soldier's general."

"What about the center attack?" said Jason.

"I told you. It has already started."

"Where?"

"Just ahead of us, in the Pindus mountains."

"Can you not hear those guns?" one of the soldiers exclaimed.

"General Papagos placed one full division of Greek Epirotes directly in front of Metsovon. They are people from this region and they have fought for hearth and home. But it has been costly. The Italians made a desperate stand at a key position on the outskirts of Metsovon and their heavy field pieces inflicted many Greek losses. Mussolini threw his crack Julia Division into the battle."

"How did the Epirotes finally make out?" asked Pavlo.

"They are stubborn mountain fighters who know every hill, every goat path in northern Greece. Their women also helped by pulling heavy guns over the treacherous mountain passes. The Italian tanks could not maneuver over this kind of terrain and within two days the Julia Division lost five thousand men. Encircled and exhausted, several thousand more surrendered rather than be killed."

"Are you trying to say that Greece won the battle?" asked one of the soldiers.

"Yes."

Pavlo belched loudly. "Now that the war is over, let us all go home."

Sergeant Michalis put his hands closer to the flames. A coldness had crept into his eyes. Jason moved away and began swinging his arms to keep warm. "Bring your blanket next to the fire," he said to Pavlo.

"Where are you going?"

"I will be right back."

"Are you going to take a shit or something?"

"No."

"Wait, I am coming with you."

"Stay here. I will be right back."

Jason walked to the shore of the lake. It was frozen. Carefully he put one foot on the ice then his full weight. It felt very strange walking on water, something he could never do in Livani.

Livani!

When he returned to the fire he found Pavlo buried under the blanket. He picked up his own blanket and eased himself into a space near the fire. In time he fell asleep.

3

Packed once again into the lorries, they were ordered out from Lake Prespa at daybreak amid loud shouts and arguments, the steady pounding of cannons in the west. It was insane, this long line of lorries moving into death. Pavlo was the only one talking. "Friends of Albania, have you ever given serious thought to how a war is conducted? It is not at all like those stories they feed us in school: three hundred Spartans at Thermopylae, Hector at Troy, Odysseus and Heracles. Fantasies and fables! A war is noise and confusion. It is the horrible smell of blood and shit."

Before setting out, Sergeant Michalis once again reminded them that they would be joining the main forces on Mount Zvezda precisely at noon. In the shadows of the mountain slopes lay the city of Koritsa, the major Italian stronghold of eastern Albania. But they had no time to stop. Rations of dry fish, bread, and cheese were distributed in the lorries. Pavlo again clamored for wine but there was none available. All along the western horizon the sky was on fire.

"You must try to eat," said Jason.

"Yes, mother."

"You have not touched a bit of food since yesterday."

"I am fasting, friend Jason."

Jason put away the cheese and bread. He tried a morsel of fish but Pavlo turned his face away. He looked more pale than ever.

"Is anything troubling you?" Jason asked him.

"I wish this damn lorry would stop!"

"Why?"

"I have to take a shit."

"The lorry cannot stop. You will have to wait."

"Then I will shit right here. I cannot hold it any longer."

"Stop thinking about it," said Jason.

The lorry started up a sharp incline and the driver had to shift gears. With an anguished cry, Pavlo slid over the side and jumped to the ground, rolling over several times. Jason pounded at the window behind the driver until he finally pulled to a halt. By this time Pavlo had finished. His face was deathly white when Jason yanked him back into the lorry.

Sergeant Michalis was seething with rage. "You crazy bastard!"

"I had to take a shit."

"Next time, do it in your pants. You heard the orders: we do not stop for anything until we reach Mount Zvezda!"

Within an hour they were in the center of Hades—British planes zooming down at Italian tanks, heavy artillery pumping shells, machine guns blasting from trenches. The moment they leaped from the lorry to scatter for the high rocks one of the men fell. He twitched and vomited blood then lay still. Jason was about to drag him toward a deep shell hole when he felt a firm hand on his shoulder. "I will take him. Go with the others."

Jason saw a uniform soiled with mud, a powerful body, thick black beard, a gold cross dangling from the neck. "Who are you?" he asked.

"I am Major Fotis."

"But I was just about to bury him in that hole . . ."

"Leave him here. I will attend to it."

Another soldier appeared. Major Fotis called him Lambro. He helped Major Fotis dig a hole with the butt end of his rifle. Jason had never seen these men before. In all the commotion he had lost sight of Pavlo. He looked everywhere but could not locate him. Frantically, he crawled away from Major Fotis and made for the high rocks just ahead.

The sky was exploding. The Greek artillery on Mount Zvezda suddenly came to life but their first volleys fell far short of their mark, almost dropping on the backs of the Spartan Battalion. Jason saw Pavlo leap from the rocks and yell, "You stupid Athenian bastards! Stop shooting at us. We are Greeks!"

Jason tugged him back into the rocks. "Why did you leave me?" he shouted.

"I thought you were right behind me," said Pavlo. "Look at those dumb Athenian bastards up there. Where the hell did they learn to fire a heavy gun, at the University?"

Lambro and Major Fotis crawled into the rocks beside them.

"Aim straight, you stupid Athenian bastards!"

"Guard your tongue," Lambro warned him.

"Why?"

"Show some respect for the cross."

"What cross?"

"Major Fotis is chaplain of our battalion."

"He is a priest?" said Jason.

"Of course."

"How were we to know?" said Pavlo.

"His insignia and cross are in plain sight."

"Where I come from, friend soldier, a priest wears a robe and a black cylindrical hat."

Another man crawled into the rocks. Major Fotis was glad to see him. "Aristides, where have you been?"

"I was cut off from you when the machine guns started in."

A sudden blast of Italian mortars sent them deeper into the rocks. Pavlo's eyes were glazed with fear. "Friend major, why do you not show your cross to God? Perhaps He has forgotten that we are on His side!"

"God will not abandon us," Lambro reproached him.

"What about the Italians, friend soldier, will God abandon them?"

At last the Athenian artillery found the range and began scoring direct hits on the machine gun emplacements. The Italians emerged into the open and started fleeing down the slope with wild cries. Pavlo tried to run away.

"Come back!" yelled Jason.

A barrage of bullets whistled over Pavlo's head and he dropped to his knees in terror. Major Fotis went after him and dragged him back to the rocks. Pavlo tried to wrestle free but he was no match for Major Fotis. Major Fotis had surprising strength. The chaplain wiped the mud away from Pavlo's face and told him to lie still and not be afraid.

Sergeant Michalis pointed toward a farmhouse at the bottom of the slope and commanded them to head for it. They waited until the machine gun blasts quieted down then scurried out of the rocks. A few hundred yards from the farmhouse they came upon a cluster of Greeks hiding behind a wall of stones. They were badly hit and disorganized. Major Fotis spoke soothingly to them while Lambro and Aristides attended to their wounds. Pavlo seemed more composed now. Jason kept a sharp eye on him.

Sergeant Michalis ordered the rest of them to continue toward the farmhouse. Two men were sent ahead. They returned moments later to report no signs of the enemy.

"We stay here for the night," said the sergeant. Sentries were posted around the farmhouse; fires were lit. The faint rumble of big guns could still be heard in the west. The first stars appeared.

They ate bean soup and bread. Jason went on sentry duty from nine to eleven. Near the barn he saw a scrawny goat sleeping on the ground. Alone under the black sky once again. No artillery or planes, no dead faces. Madness. He was a thousand miles from his home, in a foreign land, armies of soldiers at his elbow, and he knew no one but Pavlo. What was he doing with this rifle perched on his shoulder? Whom would he kill first? Who would kill him? And where was Mussolini?

When he got back to the farmhouse he found Sergeant Michalis huddled around the fire with the rest of the men. Pavlo was nervously rubbing his hands. "Friend sergeant, when are we going into Koritsa?"

"Why do you ask?"

"I can smell the women there."

"You have a big nose."

"And a big something else, friend sergeant. When are we going in?"

"At daybreak tomorrow . . ."

"Tomorrow?"

"That is what I said."

"But why wait until then? The Italians have left the city. We should not have any problems."

"Daybreak," barked Sergeant Michalis, glaring at all the men. "And we all go in together. Is that clear?"

"Sergeant, can we sleep in the house?" one of the men asked.

"No."

"Why not?"

"Because it makes a good target."

"But no one is shooting at us now."

"We sleep here by the fires. That is final."

"I saw Lambro and Aristides go inside over an hour ago."

"I sent them to look for food," said Sergeant Michalis.

"I think they have fallen asleep."

Sergeant Michalis moved closer to the fire and began, rubbing his hands vigorously. His face was like embossed leather, and always that cold hard look.

Jason drew up beside him and said, "Sergeant, do you want me to go into the house and check on those two men?"

"Go," said Sergeant Michalis, keeping his eyes on the flames.

Jason took the sergeant's flashlight and hurried toward the house. He threw the light toward the barn and saw the scrawny goat. It was still sleeping on the ground. He waited on the porch for a moment. Nothing stirred in the large front room, nor in the kitchen. Slowly, he crept upstairs but found all three bedrooms empty. He came downstairs again, passed through the kitchen then opened the cellar door. Lambro and Aristides were lying on the dirt floor next to a wooden barrel, faces stained with wine. Jason kicked them awake.

Lambro tried to get to his feet but slumped back against Aristides and began snoring again. Jason pulled them to their feet and shoved them upstairs into the kitchen. From the porch, he flashed the light to the others and beckoned them to come.

"There is wine in the cellar," he said to Sergeant Michalis.

The sergeant spat in disgust when he saw Lambro and Aristides drunk on the kitchen floor. The men pushed and shoved past the cellar door and took turns drinking from the barrel. Jason remembered the scrawny goat. He dashed into the yard and hurried for the barn. The goat was still sleeping at the same place along the side of the barn. One sharp twist of the neck and it was over. The poor creature was too weak to cry out. Pulling out his knife, he slit open the belly and dug out the entrails while two men scraped away the hair. He found a long stick, carved a sharp point at one end, then shoved it through the raw neck of the goat, pulling it past the rib cage and out through the groin. One of the men helped him tie the legs together. After this, they placed it over the fire, turning it slowly, watching it roast, but the aroma drove them all out of their minds and they started devouring the thing even before it was half-done.

4

They slept very little that night. The guns started in shortly after midnight, sending long ribbons of fire into the western sky. Most of the men slept in the cellar. Perhaps it was the wine, but Sergeant Michalis offered no objections. The place reeked from the sour odor of unclean bodies. Just before dawn Pavlo tapped Jason on the shoulder and whispered, "In a few hours we will be gorging ourselves on food and women."

"Keep your voice down," cautioned Jason.

"But I am not going to wait until then, friend Jason."

"What do you mean?"

"I am going into Koritsa now."

"Are you crazy? You heard what Sergeant Michalis said."

"To hell with him. He wants us to go in after everything is neat and clean, like a damn general!"

"Please keep your voice down."

"Friend Jason, the Italians have pulled out of the city. It is safe to go in. There is no reason to wait."

Jason tried to hold him down but Pavlo was determined. "Are you coming?" he exclaimed.

They crept past the sleeping soldiers and up the cellar stairs. There were no stars in the sky. Everything was still.

"Can you catch that scent, friend Jason?"

"Damn it, keep your voice down."

Pavlo rubbed his groin. "Did you know that Albanian women are the best lovers in the Balkans?"

Jason checked his rifle. "I just do not understand you. One

minute you are shitting all over the place, and the next . . ."

A few fires were still burning in the city. The streets were gutted with holes. Italian lorries and tanks lay on their backs, abandoned. Suddenly there was an eruption of machine-gun fire. Bullets flew over their heads. They dropped quickly to the ground and started crawling toward a crippled lorry. They waited. It was too dark to see. The shooting seemed to come from a building on the opposite side of the street.

"We have to clear out of here," warned Jason.

"And go where?"

"Back to the farmhouse."

"But what about the women?"

"You must be insane," said Jason.

They lay still until the blasts stopped. Taking a deep breath, Jason swung around the lorry and made a wild dash down the dark street. Pavlo stuck close to his heels, panting down his back as the machine guns exploded once again. When they finally came in sight of the farmhouse with its dim fire, they pulled up behind a stone wall and waited a few moments. Pavlo rolled over the ground, hurling curses at Koritsa. "You crazy Italians, could you not see that we were on an errand of mercy? Those poor Albanian women, lying there in their cold beds. Those poor Albanian women!"

• •

That afternoon the Athenian Evzones, marching in columns of three, led the victorious entry into Koritsa. The Spartan Battalion was next in line. Crowds stood along the route of march, young girls tossing flowers to the Greek soldiers, women and men weeping and crossing themselves with each peal of the church bells, one soldier breaking away from his column and scaling the roof of the city hall to pull down the Fascist flag and replace it with the Blue and White. Toward the west, the routed Italians were well on their way to Tepelini in a general retreat.

Koritsa was still smoldering. Throughout the day, the city

vibrated with speeches and martial music, and just before dusk, the loud-speakers carried the prime minister's voice from Athens:

We were attacked and forced to take up arms. We have won the first battle against the Axis, but the struggle has just begun. Greece will not die. She will live because she fights for her very existence!

They saw General Papagos for the first time, a man of exceptional height, shoulders hunched under a heavy tan coat. He spoke briefly, praising the soldiers and asking them to sustain their spirit until Mussolini was pushed into the Adriatic. People began dancing in the streets. Soldiers grabbed the young girls and kissed them despite angry protests from the mothers. Pavlo took Jason by the arm and led him into a narrow street just off the main square. He pulled him past a number of shops and down to the end of the street. They stopped in front of a small taverna. The door was partially burned and they had to kick away some stones and charred timbers to get inside. Nevertheless the place was packed with people. The proprietor spotted the uniforms and rushed forward to greet them with his short stubby arms, gleaming bald head, thick gray mustache. "It is an extreme honor and privilege to welcome you to my most humble taverna!"

"Ouzo," said Pavlo, slumping into a chair.

The proprietor let loose a second wave of hyperbole, back-slapping and praise, even the sign of the cross.

Pavlo clapped his hands impatiently. "Ouzo!"

"Of course, Afenti. I have the best ouzo, the very best."

He hurried back to the bar and brought them a bottle and two glasses, placing them down on the table with great ceremony. Jason went to pay but he was drowned by the Albanian's protests. "No, Afenti, it is we who must pay you for driving Mussolini out of our most beautiful city. When you finish with this bottle, there will be others. You are my guests, my very special guests!"

They drank against the soothing strains of mandolins, a woman's husky voice:

> *Hey, there, Benito,*
> *Hiding in that cave,*
> *Come out!*
> *At least try to be brave.*
> *The tanks and the cannonia,*
> *They are not macaronia!*

Through the cracked window Pavlo spotted a young girl peering inside. He ran out and brought her to the table. She was no more than sixteen. Her limbs were slender but her breasts were full. Pavlo could not keep his hands away from them. He offered her a glass of ouzo but before she could put it to her lips, Pavlo took the glass away and pressed his mouth to hers. When he finally released her she sucked in a deep breath, swelling her breasts even more. Pavlo was demented with passion and he kissed the girl again. She looked dazed, like someone wandering into a strange village. In the next instant, Pavlo was hurrying out of the taverna with her.

Jason felt that he should go after him, pull him away from the girl, slap his face, put him on the first train back to Kalamata. This whole thing was insane. It was easy to blame the war, far easier to blame Mussolini for dragging him into this foreign country, to kill and hate, to live like a savage with an unwashed face . . .

Ouzo! Ouzo!

The husky voice had drawn near him:

> *The tanks and the cannonia,*
> *They are not macaronia . . .*

She was at his table, leaning over him, her half-exposed

147

breasts beckoning. The crowd roared when he looked the other way. With unsteady feet, he put on his coat and stumbled out of the place.

5

Albanian winter!

The gnawing pain of hunger and sleepless nights, unbearable cold, ice-swollen rivers, invincible mountains, impassable snows; it took them one whole month to advance the short distance of twenty miles from Koritsa to Erseke. They ground their way past that little town then fought for one week to cross the Voiussa River into Permet. Like Erseke, this village too was murdered. In their frantic retreat, the Italians had destroyed everything.

Toward the north, the Greeks were moving more rapidly. Sergeant Michalis fed them all the details as they squatted around the campfires in Permet. "Four elite battalions, assisted by pack artillery, are pursuing the Italians into the mountains along the Jugoslav border. The operation is very risky. The Italians have reorganized themselves along a wide front and are being helped by steady attacks from their air force. But we have the advantage. Most of the Greeks from the four battalions live in that area. They moved their guns and equipment over treacherous goat paths and in a matter of days they have surrounded the Italians. At this very moment the bloodiest battle thus far is taking place at Pogradets."

"Where do you get all this information?" Pavlo asked him.

"From the newspapers," laughed one of the soldiers.

"How about us?" said Jason. "Where do we go from here?"

"We keep moving toward the west until we reach the Adriatic," said Sergeant Michalis.

"Meanwhile we have been stuck in Permet for three days."

"Do not be impatient. We will be moving out soon."

"When?" said Jason.

"You will be told."

Pavlo was shivering. "Friend sergeant, do we have to sleep in these damn tents tonight?"

Sergeant Michalis stretched his arms. "There are a few houses still standing in Permet. You have my permission to go there—but I want you back here at daybreak."

Pavlo's face brightened. "Come," he said to Jason.

They stopped at the first house that came into sight. It lay on the outskirts of the village. The lights were on. A nervous Albanian answered their knock and let them in. The inside of the house was unscathed but the Albanian told them his store next door had been blown to bits by an Italian bomb. His name was Naoum. His wife was twice his size, a dark obese woman whose eyes never left her two daughters throughout the entire evening meal. Anthoula was twenty and had the look of a student. Marika was eighteen, livelier, and very pretty.

After the coffee was served, Marika stepped into the front room to play a disc on an old Victrola. It was a Tsamiko dance and Pavlo quickly took hold of her hand. They danced around the divan in the front room while Anthoula sat with Jason. "Are you angry with us?" she asked.

"No."

"But you have not smiled from the moment you walked into our house."

Jason fixed his eyes on Pavlo. He was making an ass of himself, staring down Marika's bosom, acting like a horny schoolboy.

"Is it because you are away from your home?" asked Anthoula.

He gave her a taut smile.

"The Italians blew up our store last week . . ."

Jason shifted his gaze to Marika's bouncing breasts. Pavlo was whispering something into her ear which infuriated Naoum's wife, who was standing rigidly by the table, a volcano about to erupt.

"Are you married?" said Anthoula.

He shook his head.

Naoum pulled his chair close to the divan. "Afenti Jason, my mother was a Macedonian which accounts for my fair complexion. She had flaming red hair. I was baptized by a Greek priest and I shall be buried by one."

Pavlo overheard him and stopped dancing. "Why are you so anxious to call yourself a Greek?"

"Because I am proud of my heritage," said Naoum, beaming.

Pavlo scoffed. "Greece was once the cradle of democracy but look at her now. We have a figurehead of a king who, instead of leading us into battle, packed up all his treasures and fled to Crete with his family."

"Who told you this?" said Jason.

"Sergeant Michalis."

Marika changed the record to a Sirto. Pavlo asked Anthoula to dance with him. It pleased Naoum but not the thousand-eyed mother. Marika sat on the divan beside Jason. "Do you not like to dance?" she asked.

"Not now," he said.

Her lips grew sad. "Please dance with me." Unlike Anthoula, her eyes revealed a vast eagerness to share the world's love. "After tomorrow, we may never see you again."

"I do not feel like dancing," he said.

She brushed back her hair. "We have a summer house in Porto Edda. It is on the beautiful Albanian coast. Perhaps you can come with your friend and visit with us after the war."

Her mother signaled from the kitchen. Marika left him for

a moment and returned, carrying a silver tray of pastry and coffee. Pavlo stopped dancing and nudged Jason in the ribs. "Friend of America, I see that you have your gun pointed at big tits."

Jason ignited. "I am disgusted with the way you have been acting. You are a married man, the father of an innocent child!"

"Friend Jason, these are special times. Everything is permitted during war. Before you judge me, look at yourself. You have conveniently forgotten about Nikkie in Athens, the plump hen in Larissa, and now big tits here."

"I am not married. I do not have a family."

"You have the nereid, friend Jason. What would she say if she saw you with these women?"

"I am not interested in Marika," Jason stammered.

"Listen, I am not fussy. I can take the other one. We will wait until that witch of a mother falls asleep and then—do not turn your face away, friend Jason—I have everything figured out."

•   •

He wrote a long letter to Danae the next morning before daybreak. The rest of the squad was still sleeping. Under the quivering candleflame, he described the long train ride, the beauty of Edessa, Florina, Monastir. He tried to paint a picture of Albania, camouflaging the war, not mentioning the bloodshed and death, speaking only about the enormous size of the mountains, the purity of the snow, the native costumes and dances, the food. It was the first time he had written anything in two years and he had to struggle with the words. Naoum offered to dispatch the letter and after they left the Albanian's house Jason sank into a deep melancholy.

Sergeant Michalis lectured them again that morning. "The strength of the Greek Army in Albania now totals fourteen divisions. General Papagos has made it very clear that our offensive will not stop until we occupy the large naval base of Valona on the Adriatic coast. After that, Rome!"

"When are we moving out of here, friend sergeant?" asked Pavlo.

"Tomorrow morning."

"Where are we heading?"

"Argyrokastron."

"Where the hell is that?"

"About twenty miles southwest of here. It is the largest Italian supply base in Albania and lies directly on the route to Valona."

"Are the Italians going to let us take it?" Pavlo snorted.

Sergeant Michalis grimaced. "Our intelligence reports say that Mussolini has commanded his forces to defend the city at all costs. There are twenty-eight Italian divisions in this area right now, supported by three hundred fighter planes and bombers. Mussolini has gone there himself to inspect them and to direct the counteroffensive."

"So we can expect a big battle?" said Pavlo.

"Yes."

"I am getting tired of all this fighting. I wish I were in America."

They moved out of Permet early the next morning, meeting no resistance from the Italians, covering at least ten miles. At the eastern slopes of the Grammos mountains they joined forces with the main army. They had to eat on the run. Bread and cheese. Wine. The Athenian battalions led the assault, thundering down the slopes in white-hooded robes, yelling their war cry: "*Aera! Aera!*" with the Spartan Battalion following closely behind. But the Italians were deeply entrenched. Their mortar and machine-gun barrage vaulted over the heads of the white-robed Athenians, landing in the center of the Spartan Battalion. Sergeant Michalis was the first to fall, that leathery look blanched on his face, blood gushing out of his chest.

Jason knelt over him, told him not to move, but Sergeant Michalis never heard a word. As if he had dropped from the sky, Major Fotis was at their side, unscrewing the cap from his flask, tilting a few drops of brandy into the sergeant's frozen mouth. "How did it happen?" he asked.

Jason pointed toward a ledge just behind them. "Machine guns," he said.

"Mortars too," cried Pavlo.

Major Fotis scooped up a handful of snow and patted it gently over the sergeant's forehead. A stream of blood was creeping along the snow from his chest. Above them, the Italian guns were relentless. Their bullets ricocheted off snow-covered boulders, filling the sky with frightening echoes. Jason told Pavlo to follow him. They left Major Fotis with the sergeant and ran toward a clump of pine trees. A Greek unit was pinned down there. One of the soldiers saw the blood on Jason's uniform and said, "Are you hurt?"

"No."

"But you have blood on your uniform."

"It is not my blood."

A deafening concussion rocked the ground. Someone yelled, "Take care of your heads!"

The mortar barrage lasted for several minutes. Jason crawled to the trunk of the thickest pine and peered through the snow-laden branches. It took him some time to locate the position of the Italian mortars. He checked his rifle, waited a moment, then darted away from the trees and headed for the ledge. Pavlo called out to him but he kept running until he reached the wall of ledge. He crept around it cautiously and found a narrow opening in the rocks. Squirming through it, he started to climb. When he got to the top he stopped to catch his breath then put down his rifle. His heart was pounding. Carefully he crawled to the summit and looked down. A half-dozen Italians were crouched behind a barricade of sandbags.

He pulled free a grenade, waited a few seconds, then hurled it. The blast deafened him. His second grenade blew everything away, even the sandbags. Feeling numb and sick, he picked up his rifle. He could not stop his body from trembling.

Pavlo was waiting for him at the bottom of the ledge. Major Fotis was there with the whole squad. Pavlo hugged him and kissed him on both cheeks; Lambro handed him a bottle of brandy as Aristides tried to wipe the blood off his uniform with snow. A soldier with a bushy black mustache started playing a mandolin. Within seconds a circle of dancers formed around him. The rest of the squad stood off, clapping their hands and singing. He felt a lump in his throat.

Crazy Greeks, dancing and singing in the snow, the cruel Albanian winter melting on their jubilant faces, the ground sagging under the weight of their joy. Crazy, crazy Greeks.

• •

Argyrokastron did not fall easily. For two weeks the Italians put up a stubborn defense, ceaseless artillery barrages, wave upon wave of air attacks, steady mortar bombardments. The Greeks suffered heavy losses. Every night several thousand wounded were rushed to the hospitals of Ioannina but the Greek lines were never broken. When the city was finally taken, the Greeks had no time to linger. The Italians were clearly on the run now and they set out after them. Chimara. Palasi. Tepelini. With each conquered town, the sleepless British birds dipped their wings in salute.

The Spartan Battalion had just secured the town of Dukat and was about to continue toward Valona when a sudden barrage of Italian shells began dropping. The enemy was taking a stand on a rocky promontory. Word was passed to every Greek soldier that Mussolini had personally assumed charge of this assault and, like Xerxes, had positioned himself at an observation post three thousand feet above the promontory. German Stukas could be heard warming their engines, waiting to stain earth and sky with their violence.

The assault began late that afternoon. But again the Greeks held their ground, retaliating with their own heavy field pieces and mortars while the British birds took care of the Stukas. At dusk the Spartan Battalion started to move out of Dukat. There was very little left of the town. Most of its houses were demolished; the streets were cluttered with debris. Near the outskirts the men started to spread out. Pavlo was glued to Jason's side. The Italians were no longer pumping shells into the town. The Stukas could do nothing in the darkness.

Pavlo was very depressed.

"What is it?" asked Jason.

"Friend of America, do you realize where we would be if this shitty war had not started? In the name of Franklin Delano Roosevelt, we were so close, I could almost reach out and touch the Statue of Liberty!"

There was a sudden rumble of tanks.

"Two of them!" cried Jason.

"Where?"

"At the end of the street. They are heading this way."

Pavlo's face turned white.

"Quick, into that alleyway," said Jason.

They scurried into the ruins of a devastated building and wedged themselves between two large slabs of stone. The tanks started firing. Pavlo squirmed away from Jason and tried to run into a deeper opening in the stones. The tanks fired again, tearing a hole in Pavlo's stomach. Jason let out a hoarse cry and dragged him back between the two slabs. He was twitching badly and heaving blood. His face was the color of wax.

"Friend of America . . ."

"Lie still," whispered Jason.

An endless stream of blood gushed out of Pavlo's mouth. "Friend of America, when you return to Livani, go to my cellar and under an empty wine barrel you will find a package wrapped in oilskin."

"Uncle Pavlo, please lie still."

"That is the first time you ever called me uncle . . ."

"Please, try not to speak."

". . . friend Jason, I want you to have all the money inside that package. There is more than enough for you to go to America. After you get settled you can send for the others: your aunt, little Renio, your mother and father, even the nereid . . ."

He was weeping, coughing out blood and weeping.

"Friend Jason . . ."

"Uncle Pavlo, please!"

"I have always loved you, like my own brother."

"I know."

"I do not understand what came over me. I mean, with those women, and that girl in Koritsa. Do you forgive me?"

"Of course," said Jason.

"This shitty war. It ruined everything, friend Jason. Do you realize it? We were on our way to America, really on our way!"

Jason took him into his arms, tried desperately to comfort him, but Pavlo suddenly pushed him off and in a blood-splattered voice began singing:

> *Oh, say, can you see*
> *By the dawn's early light,*
> *What so proudly we hailed . . .*

Jason remembered nothing else. Another blast from the tanks sent a burning meteor through his right leg.

6

Major Fotis ministered to his wound that night. In the morning Jason accompanied him to the grave. It was on the highest hill of Dukat, on the hem of the Adriatic. Giant flakes of snow were falling. Jason's leg burned with pain. The thick bandage had come undone during the night and Major Fotis had a difficult time putting on a new one with gauze and string. He wanted a doctor to look at the wound but Jason shrugged and said he would think about it after they came back from the grave.

Major Fotis looked wan. His strong shoulders sagged as he swung the silver censer over the freshly dug hole.

> *God of all spirits and all flesh, You who have destroyed death and the power of evil, grant to your servant Pavlo a place of light, a place of peace, a place free of pain—and out of Your goodness, pardon every sin which he might have committed, either in word or deed or thought—for there is no man who has lived and sinned not.*

A debilitating weakness ate through Jason. This was Pavlo in that malignant hole, the same Pavlo who had slid through life on elusive dreams, always joking, clowning, playing the fool in a senseless world.

> *Father, accept this soldier, a noble Spartan, who loved You and honored You. Father, have mercy upon him. Christ have mercy . . .*

Time was playing tricks on Jason. Nothing was real any

longer. Only yesterday Pavlo was whole, aching to embrace America, but now he had nothing in his arms but the frigid Albanian ground.

For You are the eternal repose of Your servant Pavlo, and unto You we ascribe glory, both now and forever, and unto all ages.

Jason fed a spadeful of earth to Pavlo. The snow was coming down harder now. *What about yourself, friend Jason? What do you say about Charon? Have you forgotten how your Grandfather Andreas prayed daily for a three-day death? And before he closed his eyes after his customary glass of red wine, did he not lean forward on the bed that morning and whisper into your ear: "Good morning, my little Icarus"?*

Major Fotis put down his censer then carefully folded his embroidered stole. "Look how gently God is placing a bouquet of snow over your friend," he murmured.

"He was my uncle," said Jason.

"What?"

"He was my mother's brother."

"I am very sorry," said Major Fotis.

Jason found a thick pine branch and carved out a cross. Quickly he shoved it into the earth then stood back. It was finished. Pavlo had no more problems. He did not have to worry about shitting on the Jugoslavian landscape, about finding his way to America.

They came down from the hillside. Jason had to fight the wind and snow, the dull throb in his leg. Like vultures, huge columns of black smoke circled over Dukat. Major Fotis stopped in front of his tent and said, "Please come in. I want to talk to you."

"About what?"

Major Fotis looked at him closely. "Something."

"What is it?"

"Do you believe in God?"

Jason glanced back at the white hillside. "Above the

iconostasis of my village church is an icon of God's eye . . ."

Major Fotis became silent.

". . . when I was a child I actually believed it was God's eye. Everywhere I turned, it kept staring at me."

Major Fotis opened the flap of the tent. "Icons are mere symbols, imperfect copies of the original."

"Have you ever seen the original?" Jason frowned.

"I have seen God many times," said Major Fotis.

"What does He look like?"

"He is warmth and beauty."

Jason started to walk away.

"Are you not coming inside?" asked Major Fotis.

"No."

"But I want to talk to you."

"Some other time," said Jason.

•   •

He was racked by pain and guilt throughout the day. He wanted desperately to rejoin his unit but he did not have the heart to abandon Pavlo. He could barely stand on the leg. The bandage had slipped away from the wound and he tied it awkwardly with more string. The Greek artillery was pounding the horizon. They must have taken Valona by now. *That dreamer of a priest, talking about God in all this mess!*

At dusk he was back at Major Fotis' tent. The chaplain gave him some brown bread and a morsel of fish. From under his cot, he pulled out a bottle of red wine and poured some into two tin cups.

"Where did you get this?" Jason asked.

Major Fotis smiled. "It is for the Eucharist, but not too many soldiers take advantage of it."

"I am sorry about this morning," said Jason.

Major Fotis sipped from his cup. "Is this why you came back?"

"I kept thinking about what you said . . ."

"Go on."

". . . that you have seen God many times."

"I have." Major Fotis stood up. The wind had blown open the flap of the tent and he strapped it securely. "God is in a seed of wheat, a mother's kiss, the flight of a gull . . ."

"Is He in the grave with my Uncle Pavlo?"

"Yes."

"Gray and stinking with death?"

"Yes."

"What kind of God is He?"

"That kind of God," said Major Fotis.

Jason got up from the small folding chair and walked painfully to the flap of the tent. He peered outside. Like a busy housewife, the fierce wind was trying to sweep the world clean again; make it pure and innocent. Without looking around, he said, "It is all so ridiculous and illogical: you and I, my Uncle Pavlo, Sergeant Michalis, this damn war, God!"

"You did not touch any of the fish," said Major Fotis.

Jason spoke to the white hillside. "Have you ever thought about getting away from everything?"

"What do you mean?"

"There is a monastery not far from my village. It rests on the very crown of a high mountain. I would like to go there someday."

"Why?"

Jason did not reply.

"Do you expect to find God up there?" asked Major Fotis.

"No, I expect to find myself."

"By becoming a monk?"

Again Jason did not answer. There was a sudden explosion in his brain. *Friend Jason, what are you doing here, talking with this goatbeard? In the name of Zeus, what is this nonsense about running off to a monastery? Have you forgotten about America? You have my money. Take it and go!*

Jason returned to the chair and sat down.

"Does your leg hurt very much?" asked Major Fotis.

Jason shook his head.

"I think one of the doctors should look at it."

"No."

"At least let me change the bandage. It is almost falling off."

"Later," said Jason.

"Will you try to eat something now?"

"Yes."

Major Fotis stayed at the table until Jason finished all the fish. He could manage only half a slice of bread.

"Do you want some more wine?" asked Major Fotis.

"Yes, please."

They both fell into a long silence.

"Why did you become a priest?" asked Jason.

"For many reasons."

"Did you hear a voice calling you?"

"Yes."

"God's voice?"

Major Fotis shook his head. "It was humanity's voice, sick and suffering."

Again Jason hobbled to the flap and opened it. It was too dark to see anything now. The wind was still howling. He could not stay in one place.

"Where are you going?" asked Major Fotis.

"We must have taken Valona by now. I want to go there. I want to be with my battalion."

"I wrote to your aunt in Livani and told her about Pavlo. I think you should write to her also."

Jason's heart tightened. He took the first step down from the tent then felt the ground swaying under his feet. He slumped to his knees, fighting nausea, faintly hearing Major Fotis' voice. He tried to crawl back into the tent but his arms and legs gave in, pulling him into a pool of darkness.

•   •

He never reached Valona. For weeks he lay on his back in a small hospital outside Argyrokastron, his right leg in a cast, the pain searing his brain. Fearing gangrene, the doctors at one point were about to amputate but Jason fought it with all his strength. Major Fotis came to his assistance and begged the doctors not to operate. They shook their heads and warned that the shell fragments had not only broken the bone in several places but a large section of muscle and nerve had been torn away, and even if they did not amputate, Jason would have great difficulty walking for the rest of his life. They insisted it would be easier if they cut off the leg.

Jason began shouting at them, threatening to kill himself if they tried to do it. Major Fotis attempted to calm him but only morphine could mitigate Jason's anguish.

In the days that followed, the chaplain came repeatedly to Jason's bed. One morning he started to utter a prayer but Jason stopped him. Major Fotis returned the next day, and every day for the following two weeks. He was present when the doctors happily announced there was no necessity for amputation.

On a cold afternoon in February, Major Fotis helped Jason walk for the first time. The doctors had taken off the cast but the leg was still heavily bandaged. Jason struggled around the bed clumsily as though he had never walked before. The pain was excruciating. He took one step and then a slow pull. It exhausted him but the doctors were pleased. That night he did not touch his food. He was unable to sleep. The stark vision of himself kept hounding him: *The bell-ringer of Saint Chrysostomos, dragging his feet through the streets of Livani!*

7

The last breath of February was a day of raw anticipation and disquietude. For two hours he sat in the drafty corridor of the hospital while Major Fotis made the final arrangements for his separation papers and for the ambulance. It arrived exactly at ten in the morning and after a flurry of commotion at the main desk, nurses and doctors sped down the long hallway and returned, pushing a soldier on a wheel stretcher. He looked emaciated and hollow. He was lifted into the ambulance by two attendants. Major Fotis stood beside the rear door giving instructions and cautioning them to be careful. A few moments later he swung open the glass doors of the corridor and said to Jason, "It is time to leave."

"Where are they taking that soldier?" asked Jason.

"To a hospital in Ioannina."

"What about me?"

"These are your separation papers. Put them inside your coat and have them ready at all times. From Ioannina, you will travel by bus as far as Mesolonghi, and from there you take the ferry to Patras. The rest of your journey will be by train to Kalamata, and after that you shall have to find a way back to your village."

"I looked for you yesterday," said Jason.

"I had to be in Valona."

"Have we taken the city?"

"Yes, but our victory may be short-lived. The Germans are prepared to attack us from Jugoslavia. Hitler is disgusted with Mussolini. He wants to finish what the Italians botched up."

One of the older nurses helped him down the front steps. He had become accustomed to the cane and was able to walk by himself to the ambulance. The nurse kissed him on the cheek then opened the door. "You will sit up front with the driver," she said.

It was agony for him to pull the leg in. It seemed as though every muscle and nerve had torn open. Major Fotis carefully closed the door and stayed by the window, steaming the glass with his final words. Jason never heard them.

The ambulance swung into the street and veered southward. Jason turned and saw Major Fotis waving at him from the driveway of the hospital. God reaching out and saying good-bye, trying to blot out everything with one brush of the hand. *Pick up your feet and walk, soldier Jason. Your faith has made you whole!*

The driver was young but efficient. Jason did not bother to talk to him. It was a wild flight: the dense clouds racing across the Albanian sky, trying to keep pace with them, Pavlo crying out to him, begging him not to leave him alone. Many times the driver tried to start a conversation but Jason never responded. In less than an hour they were well past Porto Edda and on the wide road to Konispol. He should have been overjoyed to see Greek soil once again but instead he felt only a deep void when the tiny villages rolled past the window. The road became so steep and treacherous, the driver had to stop at one point and ask directions. They had gone almost ten miles before the old farmer told them they were heading east and not south.

They did not get into Ioannina until late afternoon. Jason was appalled by the sight that met his eyes. Hundreds of wounded soldiers were lying in the streets and courtyards, covered with blankets, half-frozen, waiting to be transported to other towns. "All the hospitals in Ioannina are full," explained the driver.

Jason spoke for the first time. "What about our other passenger?"

"That soldier on the stretcher? There is a bed waiting for him but I do not think he will live to make it."

He drove the ambulance directly to the front door of a large hospital that was perched on the crown of a hill. It had an expansive view of the city. The driver hurried inside then returned with two attendants who helped him pull out the stretcher. Jason did not want to look but something pulled his eyes to the gaunt body, the gray face of death. Awkwardly he lifted his hand and waved through the window but the frozen eyes saw nothing.

He dined with the driver at an inn in the heart of the city. When they came outside, the driver said, "A bus leaves Ioannina five times a day for the south."

"Are you going now?" asked Jason.

"Yes."

"Where?"

"To Valona."

"Is it true that the Germans may attack us from Jugoslavia?"

"Yes."

"What are they doing in Jugoslavia?" said Jason.

"They are prepared to launch an offensive against Russia but now they may have to wait."

"Do you think we can defeat Italy and Germany at the same time?"

The driver shook his head. "You never told me your name."

"Jason."

"And mine is Leonidas."

"Are you serious about driving back to Valona tonight?"

"Of course," said Leonidas.

"But the roads are bad. Even in the daylight we almost got lost."

"I will get there," said Leonidas cockily. He extended his hand. "Goodbye, my friend. I hope you reach home safely. I am sorry about your leg."

Watching him speed away, Jason felt an oppressive lump in his heart: one warrior lying lifeless on his shield, another driving his chariot back into battle, and he perched on one leg like a wounded gull.

He slept in the inn that night but the proprietor refused to take his money. In the morning, he explored the narrow streets of Ioannina, wandering through the shops, watching the silversmiths and jewelers work at their craft, intrigued by the casual manner of their skill. Later, he accepted an invitation from a young fisherman who took him on his small boat to the tiny island that floated in the center of Ioannina's gigantic lake. He returned in time to visit the tomb of Ali Pasha. On the road back to the inn he came upon a Byzantine church. On one of the walls inside was a flaking fresco of the philosopher Plato. Paganism and Christ under the same roof! Pavlo would have made an appropriate remark. Pavlo!

He was very tired when he got back to the inn. The proprietor served him ouzo and a glass of water then talked at length about his city, how most of her life Ioannina had endured wars, invasions, conquerors. Jason detected an eternity of suffering in the man's eyes, and yet, there was also a spirit of exultation in the way he painted Ioannina's splendor when, as the cultural center of the Ottoman Empire, she vied with Venice.

Just three cigarettes from Ioannina lay Dodona. The bus made a stop there the next morning but Jason was the only one to get out and view the remains of a once-magnificent temple to Zeus. He remembered from his schooldays that the oracle here was much older than that at Delphi, and for many centuries Dodona was considered to be the cradle of Greek civilization, but like Pavlo it too was blown away by the cold wind of death.

There were other soldiers in the bus who had got on at Ioannina but he kept away from them. One had his arm in a sling, another walked on crutches. A third acted strangely, shouting at everyone, cursing, then plunging into a pit of depressive silence. The seats in the bus were jammed close together and Jason had difficulty stretching his good leg. A gnawing pain kept biting the other.

The journey seemed endless. It appeared they would never escape the mountains. Towns whisked by like startled birds in a storm: Bizani, Kopani, Perdika, Panaghia, Kerasson, Aghios Georgios . . .

They crossed the ancient bridge into Arta. Roman arches

high above a rock-strewn river, streets and houses cloaked with snow, a sky of cold iron. The mere thought of fighting his way out of the bus tired him but when he stepped into the street his spirits were instantly lifted by the sight of coffee houses, flashing Greek eyes, volatile gestures, hands and arms arguing.

An hour later the bus was circling the Gulf of Amvrakikos, coming into Agrinion. The driver stopped here for fuel then passed some pastry around to the soldiers. At dusk they pulled into Mesolonghi.

The town was low and swampy, exactly as Lord Byron had found it. *My little Icarus, you must never forget Lord Byron. He died in the remote village of Mesolonghi, a hero who gave his life to Greece.* For one year Mesolonghi had been besieged by an overwhelming force of thirty thousand Turks—but under the command of Botsaris the Greeks were able to survive, living on courage, eating cats, dogs, even rats—and in the year 1826 plans were finally made for a massive exodus. After setting fire to the ammunition depot of the Turks, they were betrayed by one of their own villagers and only a handful managed to escape. Three thousand Greeks died in the explosions; eight thousand were tortured or raped then sold off as slaves.

There was a fifteen-minute delay while the bus driver made a brief call on one of his relatives near the center of the town. Jason took this time to visit the small house where Byron died. In a large garden a few hundred yards away, all the dead of the exodus lay buried. A sign above the iron gate read: *Garden of the Heroes.* Bitterly, Jason wished they would do the same for Pavlo; encircle an iron fence around his grave at Dukat then place a sign over it: *Here lies Pavlo of Livani who died here on his way to America.*

At Krioneri an officer of the home guard assigned him to a ferry and when he landed at Patras he hobbled to the nearby railroad station to await the train for Kalamata. It came two hours later, a slow-moving thing that made stops at every village of the Peloponnesus. They chugged into Amalias, past withered fields and tilting farmhouses.

His heart felt nothing when Taygetus came into sight. He knew he was near home when the train stopped at Kyparissia. He had come here with his father when he was twelve. His first encounter with Charon, staring at the dead face of a grandfather he had never known. A house of threnody where he saw his father cry for the first and only time.

He slept all the way from Kyparissia to Kalamata, and like a burning star, his dream plummeted toward Danae.

8

After sitting on a bench in the railroad station for more than an hour, he felt rested enough to go outside. He had to lean heavily on the cane. The leg felt stiff and numb. It was a cold day. Nevertheless the streets and sidewalks were crowded. Everyone seemed to be in a hurry. An aged farmer was approaching on a donkey. Behind him trailed a half-dozen donkeys. Jason asked him where he was going.

"To Akra, my son."

The name stabbed at Jason's memory. It was the village of the old goatherd, Themistocles, that sprinkle of white houses lying in the shadows of the monastery.

"May I ride one of your donkeys?" asked Jason.

"Of course," said the old man, pulling to a halt. He reached out and touched Jason's uniform. "Were you in Albania, my son?"

"Yes."

"What happened to your leg?"

"It was torn by shell fragments."

The old man kept his gaze on Jason's uniform. "Is it true that we pushed Mussolini into the Adriatic?"

"Yes."

"We shall lick Hitler too!"

Jason limped toward one of the donkeys, the smallest of the group.

"Where are your belongings, my son?"

"Belongings?"

"Is this how you came from Albania, without any baggage?"

"Yes."

"Where is your home?"

"Livani."

"It is not too much out of our way. We will take you there."

"That will not be necessary," said Jason.

"But look at the way you are limping. You will never make it to Livani from Akra."

"I do not want to go to Livani," said Jason. "I will be grateful if you take me to Akra."

The old man shook his head in dismay then asked him to climb on the small donkey. "My name is Barba Yianni. I have a stable in Akra, some donkeys, a few cantankerous mules. I am not a rich man but I earn a living, enough to bide my time until Charon knocks at my door. Your donkey's name is Pelopidas. He is young and gentle. Here, let me help you, my son."

"There is no need," said Jason. "I can do it myself." He braced himself on the good leg before mounting the donkey. It stood motionless until Barba Yianni gave the command to leave. Meanwhile a crowd of curious faces had gathered on the street to watch the uniform and the cane. Jason breathed deeply after he pulled away from them.

Barba Yianni was in no hurry. He drew close to Jason and said, "I forgot to ask you your name."

"Jason."

He peppered Jason with questions about the war, about Livani, his parents. They crossed two stone bridges and skirted the full length of the gulf, leaving Kalamata far behind. In the middle of the afternoon they reached a fork in the road and Barba Yianni pulled up once more with his donkey. "Are you certain you do not want us to take you into Livani, my son?"

Jason shook his head.

"That road on the left will take us there in a short time."

"What about this other road?"

"It is the way to Akra. There, you can see it in the distance."

"Do you know Themistocles?"

"Who?"

"An old goatherd named Themistocles. He told me he lived in Akra."

Barba Yianni rolled his head in sorrow. "He is not living any longer. He died several months ago. Did he tell you that he fought in the Asia Minor campaign? He was decorated by the king. Yes, Themistocles was a hero . . ."

Jason looked up toward the mountains. "How far is it from Akra to the lift?"

"What lift?"

"The one at the base of the monastery."

"The monastery? That is a good three-hour journey from Akra."

"I will pay you if you take me there."

"I am not worried about the money," said Barba Yianni.

"What then?"

"My son, I am an old man. These bones are not as strong as they used to be."

"Can you take me there tomorrow?"

"I shall have to think about it."

"I can sleep in your stable."

Barba Yianni was hurt. "Nonsense, I have another bed in my cottage. You will stay the night with me."

"But what about your family?"

Barba Yianni affectionately pointed to the donkeys. "They are my family."

His cottage was a low-slung dwelling of stucco and wood with a weather-beaten stable clinging to its side. The spacious yard was strewn with broken-down wagons, old boards, heaps of dung. More donkeys stood huddled around a wire fence; also a half-dozen mules. Everything the old man possessed seemed to be kneeling at Charon's feet.

The animals brayed loudly when Barba Yianni brought them oats and water. The mules however were not permitted to eat until the donkeys had finished. Jason walked as far as the fence and looked down at the village. There was not much to see: a dozen shabby houses, two narrow streets, an infirm church, a handful of children playing in a field.

An hour later Barba Yianni called him to the table. It was a humble meal of lentil soup and dark bread with the earth's scent still on it. Jason filled his plate twice. For some strange reason he felt comfortable here—the mules and donkeys, Barba Yianni, a sky and earth that had no attachment to the past or the future.

The animals in the yard were noisy again. Barba Yianni stirred once or twice but did not go outside. When the commotion persisted, he opened the kitchen door and let out a shrill whistle. The animals instantly became quiet. He settled back into his chair and asked Jason more questions about the war. Jason complied but after a while he noticed that the old man's eyes were half-closed.

He slept very little that night, hounded by the thought that Danae was only a few miles away. But he was not ready for her—he was not ready for Livani, for his parents, the old men at the taverna, the gawking eyes and busy tongues—not while he held this cane in his hand, not while he limped like a freak.

In the morning Barba Yianni brewed a pot of coffee, sliced some of the dark bread, toasted it over the jaki then dribbled wild honey over the slices. "Tell me," he said, "why do you want to go to the monastery?"

"Just for a visit," said Jason.

"How long do you plan to stay there?"

"I do not know yet."

Barba Yianni snickered. "You had better keep a sharp eye on those monks. They may try to put a cassock on you!"

Jason followed him into the yard. "If you are still tired I can wait until tomorrow."

"I am not coming with you," said Barba Yianni.

"I do not understand."

"Kitso will take you. He is my very best donkey and knows every step of the way."

"But how will he come back?"

"He will manage."

"By himself?"

"Of course," said Barba Yianni. He opened the gate and walked into the yard. Tossing a rope over the neck of a sturdy-looking beast, he pulled it toward Jason. The donkey had a gentle disposition and Jason mounted it without any difficulty. Barba Yianni hurried into his cottage and came back with some cheese and bread neatly wrapped in a white cloth. "It is a very hard climb up those mountains, my son. You will get hungry along the way." With this, he stooped over and began chanting into the donkey's ear: "*Kyrie eleison, Kyrie eleison, Kyrie eleison!*"

"What are you doing?" said Jason.

"I am telling Kitso the road. When I chant *Kyrie eleison* he knows that I want him to go to the monastery. Now if you had asked to go to Kalamata I would have slapped my heel and yelled *'Opa!'* Kitso is my smartest donkey." He gave the animal a hard slap on the rump but it remained stationary. Another slap. "Forward, Kitso. You ate well, you drank, and now you must work. *Kyrie eleison, Kyrie eleison!*"

Flipping back its ears, the donkey brayed then slowly moved out of the yard, Barba Yianni sticking close to its side, slapping it tenderly on the rump and chanting: *"Kyrie eleison, Kyrie eleison!"*

Jason leaned over to thank him when they came into the street but Barba Yianni was still engrossed with his chanting. They had almost passed through the entire village before he finally stopped and trudged back to his cottage.

The donkey astounded Jason. Even after they had left Akra it threaded its way with sure feet through slippery ravines and up high cliffs, passing layer upon layer of greenstone that sparkled against huge pillars of rock. For the first time Jason became aware of the wind swirling furiously around his head, picking up small stones and broken olive branches, hurling everything against the strong feet of Taygetus. By midday they had cut across a rising plateau speckled with scrub pines and wild olive trees. A cluster of cypresses was at prayer, bowing low and acknowledging the wind's supremacy. They entered a deep gorge where Jason stopped to rest. He tried to slide off the donkey but his right leg got caught on the rope and he fell backwards, landing on a bed of stones. He was not hurt. A small stream was flowing through the gorge and he crawled to it and drank.

It was an arduous task to get back on the donkey. The rocks were wet and his leg kept slipping but the gentle animal seemed to understand and it did not move until he succeeded. Within an hour they were surrounded by immense cone-shaped boulders that tottered precariously on the edge of high cliffs. The donkey slackened its pace, taking cautious little steps and sometimes backing away to a better path. Jason unwrapped the white cloth and started eating. He placed some bread and cheese in front of the donkey's mouth but it pulled its head away and brayed.

They continued up the sharp path of rocks until they reached a place that jarred Jason's brain, the slab of stone where he and Danae sat—that same cliff where Themistocles stood, pointing his bony finger toward the gray walls of the monastery. Soon they were immersed in a new world of mountains. Pale shafts of sunlight pierced through the mile-high spikes of rock as the donkey tried to maneuver its steady little feet toward the rising plateau of white bedrock. In its center stood an old wooden shelter with a half-broken sign nailed to one of its posts. Jason could barely make out the words: *To signal the monastery, strike the bell three times and then step into the cage.*

The bell was hanging from the branch of an aged pepper tree next to the shelter. A few paces to the left, and directly below the towering precipice, lay a straw cage large enough for a man to stand in without striking his head. Tied securely to the center post of the cage was a strong rope.

Jason carefully slid off the donkey. He stretched his neck and arms, rubbed his shoulders. The leg felt numb but strangely it was not hurting him. He came beside the donkey and patted it on the rump, nudging it away. "Go back, Kitso. Go back to Barba Yianni. Barba Yianni!"

He felt silly talking like this but the donkey's ears stiffened, the tail swished, and after a series of loud brays, it moved off, swallowed by the darkening rocks. He waited a moment then hobbled to the cage. He could not get Danae out of his mind. He tried not to think about Koritsa and Argyrokastron, about that lonely grave on a hill at Dukat.

He struck the bell several times then stepped into the cage. Pavlo's voice instantly thundered in his ears: *In the name of reason, where are you going, friend Jason? That is not the way to America!*

He closed the door quickly and latched it to the leather strap that hung on the side. The rope grew taut, stretching toward the sky, pulling the cage, scraping it over the ground, kicking up dust until it finally hung in the air, swaying and dipping with the wind, coming close to the hard precipice but never striking it, climbing, climbing, an invisible hand reaching down from the chambers of space, lifting him into a new world, higher, higher, into purity and freedom, into peace.

FIVE

Four figures in black habits and cylindrical hats were pulling at the rope, guiding the cage over the top of the rocky summit, bringing it to rest beside a windlass, without commands, without any exchange of words. One of them came forward and opened the door of the cage. "My name is Brother Petros," he said. "Welcome to the Monastery of the Living Blood." He was several inches taller than Jason, with the arms and shoulders of an Atlas. The other men did not speak.

Jason's head was still spinning and he tried to steady himself before stepping out of the cage. He gave the giant monk his name and then stood aside while all four began lowering the cage down the precipice. After the cage touched bottom, Brother Petros motioned Jason to follow them down from the summit. He took one step, slipped on a stone and almost fell.

A demented wind was digging a tunnel through his ears. He struggled to his feet and caught up to the monks at a very steep path that cut through a corridor of rocks. He had to stop several times to rest his leg and although the monks never looked back he managed to stay within sight of them. The wind had the strength of a thousand horses, howling and pushing, threatening to blow everything off the mountain.

At last they crossed a wooden bridge that led into a quadrangle bordered with dwarf fruit trees. Overhanging balconies were painted in bright gaudy colors. Several mules were tethered in one corner, their heads buried in canvas food bags, their little bells tinkling from their necks, breaking the silence. White birds flitted in and out of a small pool filled with water while others perched daintily on the branches of the fruit trees.

It was a child's world, bright and gay, colors everywhere, animals and trees, mysterious figures in black robes and hats passing through the arched porticoes, a music-box chapel. Jason was mesmerized. Above him, the sun sparkled, throwing its rays into the quadrangle, investing everything with a divine hue. The four monks had walked away, leaving him alone. After a few moments, a sprightly old monk approached him. "Welcome, my son. I am Brother Timotheos, hosteler of the monastery."

Jason told him his name.

"How long do you plan to stay with us?"

"I do not know," said Jason curtly.

The aged face smiled. "We rarely have guests in the winter. Why are you wearing that uniform?"

"I have just returned from Albania."

"You were in the war?"

"Yes."

A current of pain passed across Brother Timotheos' face. "Were you hurt badly?"

"I was hit by shell fragments from the turret gun of a tank," said Jason.

"That is a very heavy cane. How long shall you need it?"

"I do not know."

The old monk shuddered. "Come, I must show you around the monastery before we lose the light. Darkness falls quickly upon high places." He escorted Jason across the quadrangle and stopped at a staircase below the balconies. "That red door upstairs leads into our reception room. Follow me, my son. Be careful. These stairs are very narrow."

Jason hesitated.

"Is anything wrong?" asked Brother Timotheos.

"No."

The hosteler was very agile and even seemed impatient to

get to the top of the stairs. After reaching the last step, Jason stopped to rest. The red door brought them into a room of glossy blue walls, old furniture, yellowed photographs of monks and abbots, a gigantic icon of the Virgin. Brother Timotheos stepped into an adjacent room and came back with a plate of orange peel preserve and a large glass of water. He nodded his head approvingly when Jason finished eating. At that moment, the room vibrated from the loud clang of a bell.

"Vespers," said Brother Timotheos. He assisted Jason down the narrow staircase, holding him tightly by the arm until they crossed the quadrangle. The sun was still streaking down at them when they entered the small chapel. One by one, the monks proceeded to the iconostasis to venerate Christ and the Virgin. From there, they stopped before a very old monk sitting in a wooden chair. After prostrating themselves in front of him, they stood up and kissed his hand.

The service began.

Everyone remained standing. Ribbons of candlelight danced along the walls, inflaming the stained-glass windows. The faces of the saints on the iconostasis were cracked and faded with age. A mosaic of Christ the Pantocrator consumed the entire dome.

The monks chanted in unison. Jason had never heard music like this. It was as though he had awakened from a deep sleep and found himself in a place pulsating with gold and silver, shapeless notes floating on delicate wings, linked together and stretching gracefully toward the roof of the universe. He was reluctant to leave the chapel, even after all the monks had filed slowly into the quadrangle.

Brother Timotheos again took him by the arm. When they came to the small pool the old monk stopped. He took a few steps toward the dwarf fruit trees then reached out his hand and tenderly touched one of the white birds. It made no effort to fly away. Brother Timotheos moved his hand to another bird and began stroking it on the breast. "These white friends came to us in the heart of winter many years ago," he murmured.

Jason was astounded. "Do they ever fly away?"

Brother Timotheos shook his head. "They have no desire to fight either the wind or the outside world. They are content to remain here, never venturing beyond these trees or the pool."

"What kind of birds are they?"

"We do not know. We call them the birds of winter."

Jason turned away in anger. *They were endowed with wings and they did not want to fly.*

The quadrangle was cloaked with shadows. He breathed easier when he discovered that the refectory was on level ground, free of stairs. They entered a long rectangular hall with heavy oak tables and benches, fresco-covered walls. The monks had their heads bowed but Jason noticed the giant Brother Petros staring at him.

"Sit down, my son," said Brother Timotheos, pointing to a vacant bench.

Throughout the meal, a young monk read from a lectern that was set on a high platform. His voice echoed against the walls of the refectory: "And they came unto the other side of the sea, into the country of the Gadarenes, and when he was come out of the ship immediately there met him from out of the tombs a man with an unclean spirit who had his dwelling among the tombs. And no man could bind him, neither could any man tame him. And always, night and day, he was in the mountains and in the tombs, crying and cutting himself with stones. And he asked him: 'What is thy name?' And the man answered, saying: 'My name is Legion . . .'"

The sky had given birth to a million stars when they came outside. An infant moon was crawling over the dome of the chapel. Leaning on the arm of Brother Timotheos, Jason climbed the unfriendly stairs once again then braced himself against one of the tables while the hosteler showed him the library and each of the glass cabinets that preserved ancient manuscripts and hundreds of leather-bound tomes. "We once housed more than three hundred monks here," said Brother Timotheos sadly. "But now we are less than sixty. We grow old and die, and only a few come to take our place."

"Do the monks ever speak to each other?"

The hosteler folded his thin arms. "Only when it is necessary. Speech is entirely forbidden during the period of the Long Silence. As hosteler, I am permitted to speak to visitors. The same holds true for the abbot."

Jason leaned on the cane and walked to the door.

"Does silence bother you, my son?"

"At times."

"You will get accustomed to it. But I am afraid no one gets accustomed to that raving beast outside. I am speaking of Boreas. When he sweeps down at us from his lair in Macedonia we flee into our cells. I have seen him tear away trees, dislodge great boulders, and send them crashing down the mountain like tiny pebbles."

They returned to the balcony. "The abbot's quarters are nearby," said Brother Timotheos. "Father Athanasios will be pleased to see you."

They passed along the cells and stopped before a double door. Brother Timotheos knocked softly. He did not wait for a response. Pushing the door open, he beckoned Jason into an oak-paneled room whose center was dominated by a large mahogany desk. Bookshelves were everywhere. A white-bearded man arose from behind the desk and came forward to greet him. He was the same monk before whom all the others had prostrated themselves at the chapel.

In a delicate but firm voice, he spoke about the world of noise and the world of silence. The words flowed effortlessly as though from a deep well: vague pronouncements about forms and ideas, Plato, the cave, the light. "Peace is the one thing we can offer you, my son. During your stay here you will eat with us, chant with us, meditate with us. In the beginning, you may feel out of place, knowing that you are cut off from the other world, but in time the seeds of peace will take root in your heart."

Unfamiliar names swarmed into Jason's brain: Tolstoi, Dante, Voltaire, Shakespeare, Goethe—but like a powerful magnet the aged voice kept pulling him back to Plato—and after a long moment of silence everything was placed in the lap of Christ, not the miracle worker or magician, but Christ the Scholar.

This was not Pappa Sotiri, nor Major Fotis. There was no human identification to this voice. It had nothing in common with a world of frenzied activity, human greed, lust, suffering, and death. Everyone and everything was stripped down to nothing. Only the thought remained, the idea. And it was perfect.

Back once again on the balcony, they passed by the cell doors. Some of the monks were chanting. Below them, the quadrangle lay perfectly still, lamps flickering, God breathing. Brother Timotheos opened a door and invited him inside. It was a simple room, primitive but clean. It had a lumpy bed, a table, a chair, a brazier, a kerosene lamp. Brother Timotheos started a fire in the brazier and stood over it until the flames matured. Hurrying across the floor, he picked up a large brass bucket from the corner of the room and brought it to Jason. There were bones inside it, human bones: a skull and other pieces, gray and decaying. "These are the remains of Brother Simeon," he declared with reverence. "He occupied this cell for thirty-eight years. All the other cells have similar memorials. When I am rewarded with eternal peace my bones will be stored here also."

Jason put his hands over the brazier.

"If we are constantly reminded of death," Brother Timotheos added, "we will never fear it."

Fingers of icy rain were scratching at the window. The

room still felt cold. Brother Timotheos threw more coals into the brazier. Jason wished that he would leave. He yearned to be by himself. There were many things on his mind. His legs still felt unsteady. What was he doing here? He could not believe it or understand it. What insane hand brought him here? A spontaneous panic gripped him. He was trapped. That cage was his only means of escape.

"This is my cell," said Brother Timotheos, "but I want you to have it. The sheets are clean. I changed them only this morning."

"I do not want to take your cell," said Jason.

The old monk insisted. "We are all renters here on earth. Nothing is ours. Everything belongs to God." He opened the door and stepped into the balcony. "There is a chamber pot beneath the bed. It will spare you a trip to the water closet in the quadrangle. Try to sleep, my son. You look very tired. We shall meet again soon."

At last he was alone. Eventually the room got warm. The rain was coming down harder. He took off his heavy coat and sat on the edge of the bed. He tried to rub the numbness away from his leg but it was impossible. Slowly he rolled up his trouser to look at it. It was a blotch of red, an unsightly mound of wrinkled skin. He rolled down the trouser and stretched out on the bed. A faint rumble of thunder echoed through the pelting rain, reminding him of Dukat.

A deep sleep possessed him.

•   •

He was awakened by a soft tinkling sound outside his door. The kerosene lamp had gone out, the room was cold. He reached for his cane and stumbled to the door. It was Brother Timotheos, his thin silhouette projected against the lights in the quadrangle. "It is time for midnight prayers," he whispered, stepping into the cell.

Jason groped for the kerosene lamp.

"We do not need any light," said the old monk. The fire in the brazier had gone out. He lit it then walked toward the window. Lifting his head, he spread out his arms and intoned: "Oh, Lord, You are great. You are clothed with honor and majesty. You cover Yourself with light, unfold the curtains of heaven, lay the beams of Your chamber in the waters, make the clouds Your chariot, walk upon the wings of the wind . . ."

Jason stared into the crackling flames until Brother Timotheos came away from the window. The monk touched him tenderly on the head. "My son, I hope you decide to stay with us a while, at least until the first rays of peace enter your heart."

2

He immersed himself in the slow unraveling of days, in endless questions without answers, long walks with Brother Timotheos, the ethereal chant of the monks, the song of Plato from the lips of Father Athanasios. But it was Brother Timotheos who touched his heart the most.

"My son, the life of a monk is not easy. We are awakened from sleep at ten o'clock every night and immediately do penance through prostrations, prayers, and meditations. I have seen monks prostrate themselves up to five hundred times a day. I try to do at least one hundred. Throughout these prostrations we constantly recite the Jesus Prayer."

"What is that?" asked Jason.

" 'Lord Jesus Christ, have mercy upon me!' " And to the Virgin, we say, 'Most Holy Mother of God, save me!' At two in the morning the semantron sounds and we all go to church. There is nothing more beautiful than the early morning prayer. The soul is most tranquil at this time, most receptive to God. After this, we partake of our first meal. If it is a fast day we have camomile tea, dry bread, jam, and olives. On other days we eat cheese, vegetables, milk, and bread. We always have soup on hand. We then sleep for three or four hours and when we arise we are obliged to perform various chores. Some work in the kitchen, others in the refectory, the church, the bakery, the gardens, the infirmary. Before undertaking any task we cross ourselves and do several prostrations. Our work schedule lasts about four hours and at three in the afternoon the bell sounds for vespers, and here again begins the period of Long Silence which is followed by our second and last meal. Our day ends with the Great Canon to the Virgin."

Jason was only half-listening.

". . . I forgot to mention confession. It is imperative that each monk find a trusted confessor. Once he does, he must never hold back one word, one thought. If we are not ashamed to commit sin, we should not be afraid to confess it."

Half of February was eaten and already the days were growing longer. The ground in the quadrangle felt soft under their feet and the white birds were singing in the barren fruit trees. "It is a good day for a walk to the summit," said Brother Timotheos. He led the way out of the quadrangle and up the long corridor of rocks. An insane wind greeted them at the windlass. Somewhere in the mist below lay Livani. The thin lines of Kalamata stretched across the horizon.

They could not stay on the summit because the wind was too much for them. Jason followed the old monk down the corridor of rocks. Brother Timotheos swerved to the left just before they reached the wooden bridge. After a few minutes they proceeded slowly down a gradual slope and came into a sheltered valley that was dense with wild olive trees. They sat on a fallen trunk to rest. Jason's leg was throbbing. He massaged it with both hands and then asked Brother Timotheos, "How many years have you been at the monastery?"

"Forty-one, this coming Easter."

"Did you ever have any regrets?"

"Regrets?"

"The loneliness has never bothered you?"

"Not if I engross myself in God, not if I constantly say to myself: 'I am nothing. I seek nothing.'"

"What about your other needs?" said Jason.

"I have learned to curb them."

"Even when you were a young monk?"

"It was more difficult then, much more difficult." A twinkle flashed into Brother Timotheos' eyes. "Euripides thanked God for endowing him with old age. It placed no further demands on his carnal obligations."

Jason peeled a strip of bark from the trunk. "But is it enough, praying all day, all night, never talking to anyone?"

The old monk's knees cracked when he stood up. "The spiritual life is not all stillness and repose. The awareness of God does not come easily and without a price. It is an endless struggle but if we are diligent we shall succeed. We must never lose sight of the fact that God moves all things, unbinds all things . . ."

"Can He unbind the lameness from this leg?" said Jason bitterly.

Brother Timotheos shook his head with emphatic denial. "In His eyes you have no lame leg. He sees only perfection and beauty. My son, we live in an imperfect world. This is not a mountain, a real mountain. That is not a real sky. Everything we see with human eyes or touch with human hands is but a poor imitation of the real."

"What then is real?"

"Only the things of the spirit."

Jason felt a depressive exhaustion. What was he doing on this mountain, discussing the real and the unreal with an old man whose days and nights were numbered? What did he expect to find?

"It may take a lifetime," Brother Timotheos continued. "Or even eternity, but in the end we must all envision ourselves as perfect, just exactly as God envisions Himself. This is the great challenge of the spiritual life: to transform the imperfect into the perfect."

Jason picked up his cane. He did not call upon it all the way out of the valley but when they reached the slope he had to use it once again. Nevertheless he was exuberant. Perhaps the leg was getting stronger after all. His joy was short-lived. When they crossed the old wooden bridge his leg got caught on one of the planks and he almost fell. Brother Timotheos was walking ahead and did not see him. In the quadrangle he took Jason by the arm and said, "When we visit with Father Athanasios tonight you can ask him those same questions. I am certain he will give you better answers."

• •

A freezing rain fell on the mountain that night and when the semantron sounded Brother Timotheos failed to appear. Jason was anchored in thought. Through the icy splashes on the window he looked down at the quadrangle and saw thin slivers of lamplight reflecting against each wall. The wind was bending the mountain. Eaten with restlessness, he picked up the cane and walked out of the cell. The balcony was slippery and shaking from the wind. He had to use the cane and the railing. Passing by the row of cells, he could hear the familiar drone of the monks at prayer. One of the doors was open and he caught a fleeting glimpse of huge Brother Petros sitting in a chair, eyes closed and murmuring. Further down, and also from an open cell door, a soft melodious strain touched his ear. He stopped at the threshold and glanced inside. It was the same monk who read at the refectory when he first arrived at the monastery.

He wanted to linger there and listen to the music but he felt uncomfortable, intruding on the monk's hour of privacy. He took several steps and abruptly the chanting stopped. A voice reached out to him: "Please do not go away."

"I do not want to disturb you," said Jason.

The young monk was at the threshold. "You are not disturbing me. Come inside. You will get soaked out there."

"I was drawn to your voice," Jason stammered.

The monk motioned toward the straw chair near the kerosene lamp. "I am Brother Antonios," he said, offering his hand to Jason. It felt soft and delicate. "I learned from Brother Timotheos that you were in Albania."

"Yes," said Jason, sitting down.

"Does your leg hurt very much?"

"At times."

The eyes twinged with anguish. "Where is your home?"

"I live in a small village not too far from here. You can see it from the windlass on a clear day."

"Are you going back to Albania?"

Jason shook his head.

"Then why are you wearing that uniform?"

"I have no other clothes."

"That is a sturdy cane you are holding."

"The chaplain of our battalion gave it to me. It is made of walnut."

"We never have visitors in the winter. What brought you here?"

Jason did not answer.

"You seem very quiet. Is anything on your mind?"

Jason studied the tiny flames in the brazier. "I was told that the monks are not permitted to speak during the period of Long Silence."

Brother Antonios smiled. "That is true. But it is almost impossible to pass through each day without uttering a word or two, especially if one is young. The older monks are easily given to silence because their minds dwell constantly on death."

"Was it difficult to learn the chant?" asked Jason.

"Yes, in the beginning."

"Did it take a long time?"

"When one loves something he does not measure its growth."

"Do you think you could teach me?" said Jason.

The eyes opened wide with surprise. "You want to learn the chant?"

"Yes. Would you teach me?"

"I think so."

"When could we start?"

"Whenever you say. But it depends . . ."

"On what?" asked Jason.

"The chant cannot be learned overnight. How long do you plan to stay with us?"

"I do not know."

Brother Antonios hunched his shoulders. "It is unimportant. We can at least take the first step. Do you want to come here after the ten o'clock prayers?"

"Yes."

"Good. Perhaps now you can answer my question."

"What question?"

"Why did you come to this monastery?"

"I cannot explain it. Maybe it was my curiosity."

"Could you not have satisfied this curiosity in the summer when the weather is more inviting?" Brother Antonios smiled.

Jason laughed.

The eyes became serious. "I think we should not regard this as a visit of curiosity. Everything we do, everything that is done to us is decreed by God. It was His hand that brought you here."

Jason squirmed in the chair.

"Have you ever given thought to becoming a monk?" asked Brother Antonios.

Jason laughed.

"Perhaps you should. Yes, it is a rigid life, full of hardship and deprivation, but if you endure you gain the sweet victory of spiritual fulfillment. During the course of the novitiate you would discover that the words *vigilance* and *watchfulness* appear twenty-two times in the New Testament. This is precisely why the monk never sleeps more than three hours at a time. 'Behold, I come quickly,' says our Lord, 'even as a thief in the night. And blessed is he whom I find watchful . . . and unworthy is he whom I find slothful and asleep!' "

"I have no intention of becoming a monk," said Jason sharply.

Brother Antonios was enthralled by his own words. "Another thing, sin thrives on a full belly. Unless we fast, we all fall victims to desire. There is no quicker road to destruction than physical desire. By weakening the body we strengthen the soul . . ."

Jason pushed himself up from the chair.

"Nothing of a female nature is allowed in this monastery," Brother Antonios plowed on. "No female cats, dogs, goats, sheep. No chickens, no sows, not even female saints or angels. Every female is excluded except the Mother of God. She reigns supreme."

Jason walked to the door.

"Are you offended by what I said?" asked Brother Antonios.

Jason spun around. "I do not understand how you can do it."

"What?"

"Deny yourself all these things."

"What things?"

"Proper food on the table, a woman's body . . ."

Brother Antonios walked to the window and gazed into the darkness. "When I first came here it was very difficult, especially at night, sitting alone in this cell, thinking about my family in Kalamata, my friends—but in time I managed to overcome it."

"How?"

Brother Antonios did not answer. Slumping to his knees, he started beating his chest. Jason became alarmed and scrambled toward him. He bent over and tried to pick him up but the monk, oblivious to his presence, began intoning in a quaking voice: "Unto Thee, oh Lord, do I lift up my soul. Oh, my God, I trust in Thee. Let me not be ashamed. Let not mine enemies triumph over me!"

3

The next morning he and Brother Antonios walked to the valley of the wild olive trees on the southern slope of the mountain. The vineyards were spread out beyond the trees and halfway up an adjacent slope. Flocks of partridges pecked at the barren vines. A tiny stream passed quietly through the olive trees. They sat near its edge and Brother Antonios started explaining the chant. His voice became so impassioned Jason feared he would fall into another fit.

"The chant has eight modes, four major and four minor. We shall begin with the First Mode, the queen. All the others are based on this." Maneuvering his voice over the notes with grace and ease, Brother Antonios went on to explain the intricate identifications of the mode, the particular tone-endings, the golga and trigolga, the breathings, the range of scale. From there, he passed to the Second Mode, chanting from the same psalm of David but using different endings, a different range of notes. After an hour he had covered the first four modes.

Before Jason could digest them, Brother Antonios plunged into the Plagian Modes. "It is here that the chant becomes most beautiful," he exclaimed. He used no book, no written source. Everything came from memory: long passages from David strung together in an aura of mystery, pauses and inflections, soaring strength and subtle beauty. Jason wished he would continue forever but after another hour the monk stood up. "If you want, we can continue tomorrow," he said.

"I will never manage this music," said Jason. "It is too difficult."

"You must be patient. First, you have to familiarize yourself with every note of the scale. After that, we will proceed to the First Mode, only the First Mode. In time we will get to the more difficult Plagian Modes."

"Before we go," said Jason, "can we talk about last night?"

"Last night?"

"You frightened me, the way you were kneeling on the floor and striking your chest."

Brother Antonios fidgeted with his hands. "We are always beset by temptations—a spoken word, a gesture. We must forever be on guard against the Evil One."

"The devil?"

"He is constantly trying to ensnare us . . ."

"Surely, you do not believe this?"

"He comes in various forms and disguises," exclaimed Brother Antonios, his eyes widening. "We must be diligent!"

"There is no truth to what you are saying," retorted Jason. "You are paying credence to fear and superstition."

"No, the Evil One really exists!"

Jason looked at him closely, alarmed by his gauntness. It seemed that only a strand of prayer held him together. "Is this a fast day?" he asked him.

Brother Antonios shook his head.

Jason snapped off a strong branch from one of the pine trees and whittled it carefully with his pocket knife. He took off his elastic belt, cut out two strips, and tied them securely to each point of the sling. He tested it several times for strength.

"What are you doing?" said Brother Antonios.

"I do not want to ensnare you with another temptation," replied Jason. He picked up a small stone and put it into the crotch of the sling. Brother Antonios started to say something but Jason asked him to remain quiet.

Moving away from the monk, he leaned on his cane and walked toward the vineyard. After finding a suitable place, he hid beneath the spotted shadows and waited. A few minutes went by before he heard a flutter of wings. A partridge, full and round, perched itself on a vine above him and began nibbling at its tiny sprouts. Slowly, he drew aim. Just as he was about to release the stone Brother Antonios grabbed him by the arm and threw the sling to the ground. "You intended to kill that bird!" he cried.

Jason picked up the sling. "I was doing it for you."

"For me?"

"Look at yourself. You are skin and bone. You cannot survive on prayer and meditation."

Brother Antonios was trembling. "I never expected you to do such a cruel thing. You really wanted to kill that bird!" He pulled the sling away from Jason and broke it in two. Again Jason tried to explain, but by this time Brother Antonios had disappeared into the maze of olive trees.

4

For weeks he was torn between peace and disquietude. Danae haunted him in his sleep, enticing him with her softness, and when he awoke he was drained, his body and bed soaked with sweat and seed. But despite his agony he was grateful for discovering the wondrous joy of magnificent notes strung together in a pure embrace, clinging to mystery and enchantment. Under the daily tutelage of Brother Antonios, he managed to learn all the modes of the Byzantine chant and was now able to attach the music to the psalms of David, the songs of Solomon, the prophecies of Isaiah.

He was most exuberant during the early hours of morning when he chanted alone beneath the dim glow of the kerosene lamp, without the assistance of Brother Antonios. It was like walking without the cane. *My little Icarus, you must take each note and put wings to it, send it flying into the ear of God.*

Brother Timotheos called on him early one morning. Jason had not seen the old monk for more than a week. He did not look well.

"Have you been ill?" Jason asked.

"I caught a chill and Brother Eugenios insisted that I be confined to the infirmary until the fever passed."

"How do you feel now?"

"Fine. Would you like to walk to the summit with me?"

"But that would be too arduous for you," said Jason.

"On the contrary. It will do me good. It is a clear day and quite mild. Come."

Jason picked up his cane and followed Brother Timotheos down the narrow stairs into the courtyard. After crossing the wooden bridge, Brother Timotheos remarked, "I have detected a new light in your eyes, my son, something you did not have when you first came here."

"I have learned all the modes of the chant," said Jason.

"That is incredible. It usually takes years. Brother Antonios must be a good teacher."

When they reached the windlass, Jason walked to the edge of the summit and looked down. Livani was plainly visible — the church, the quay, the harbor. Brother Timotheos came beside him and said, "The chant is like the breath of God, so pure and divine. I am thrilled that you have grasped it in only a matter of weeks."

"There is still much more to learn," said Jason.

Brother Timotheos touched him on the arm. "Your eyes are fastened to something below. What is it, my son?"

"I can see my village—there, on the edge of the sea."

"Do you miss it?"

Jason did not reply.

"Have you decided to return there?"

"I am not ready to go back."

"Why not?"

"I do not know the reason."

"How long do you think you can postpone it?"

Jason moved away from the edge and walked back to the windlass. Brother Timotheos stuck close to him. "My son, it is impossible to run away from life. It has an uncanny way of finding us no matter where we go. Let me tell you something: I never wanted to be a monk. In my heart, I desired to go to Athens and study philosophy but I was very poor and we had a large family, so I compromised and came to this monastery. It made no demands for money. But above all, I had a place to sleep and food on the table. Only after many years had passed did I finally understand that I found what I was really seeking: the philosophy of God which transcends human wisdom."

"Then in a sense you too ran away?"

"Every soul in this monastery has run away from something, even our white birds. But have we really escaped? If we were suddenly thrust into the world we could never take care of ourselves and surely we would die."

"Then what is the solution?"

"Is it not clear to you that we all create prisons for ourselves? Only death can make us free."

"I want to think about life," said Jason angrily. "Why must everyone in this monastery surround himself with death?"

"Because it is inevitable."

"So is life."

"My son, life is nothing but a symbolic drama. Everything we experience must represent to us a deeper, more mystical meaning. Life is not bone and muscle. It is the soul confined in the tomb of the body. The only way it can be liberated is through death."

"I do not want to hear this," cried Jason. He spun around and started down the corridor of rocks. Brother Timotheos caught up to him at the wooden bridge. "Perhaps you are right, my son. I am sorry. You are young. Your thoughts should not dwell on death."

The wind was kicking up again, sending cold blasts down from the sky. Jason took off his coat and threw it over the shoulders of Brother Timotheos. The old monk laughed. "It appears that God has another breath. *Boreas*. Listen to him, my son. Is he not frightful?"

Before entering the quadrangle, Jason stopped and said, "What if I decided to stay here?"

"You mean, become a monk?"

"I have walked with you, eaten with you, and now I have learned the chant. For weeks I have done what every monk has done."

"Except one thing," said Brother Timotheos gravely. "You have not put on a monk's habit. You have not taken a monk's vow."

Jason fell silent.

"My son, if God wanted you to be a monk He would have called you."

A river of gall flooded into Jason's veins. What was he doing to this old monk, leading him on like this, asking all these foolish questions, camouflaging his real feelings? How could he tell this spotless man of God that his only imprisonment was a torturous desire for soft flesh, for Danae's thighs and breasts, her moist lips, the warmth of her arms?

"No, my son, you must go back to your village. The prison of the world does not hold the same terror as the inner prison, the prison of fear and guilt. But there is no hurry. Stay with us a while longer. As the days unwind, you will be enraptured by your progress. The new birth will take root in your heart when you least expect it. Watch over your thoughts. If you think fear, you will be fearful. If you think peace, you shall abide in it. And when the day finally comes for you to leave, you will be ready."

•   •

A heavy snow fell on the mountain that night. Through the window of his cell, Jason watched one of the monks light the oil lamps at each corner of the quadrangle. He went about it with great care and when he was done the golden beams spread like molten steel over the snow. Jason walked away from the window and sat on his cot. He tried to concentrate on the pages of music that Brother Antonios had left with him earlier in the afternoon but his mind kept racing to Danae. He got up once again and started pacing around the cell.

There was a knock on the door. He opened it and saw the huge form of Brother Petros, his cassock and brown beard blown back by the fierce wind. "I have wanted to visit with you several times," he said, "but you are always in the company of Brother Antonios."

Jason offered him the chair.

"I understand that you have learned the Byzantine chant."

Jason smiled. "I know the modes but there is still much more to learn."

"You must love music."

"I do."

"My father was the first chanter in Sparta," said Brother Petros, getting up from the chair.

"Where are you going?" asked Jason.

"I cannot stay. I must go to the library."

"But you just came in."

The monk reached for the doorknob. "I have been copying from a manuscript that dates back to the seventh century. Did you ever hear of Barnabas?"

"No," said Jason.

"Like Philo and Origen, he is very symbolic . . ."

The names dangled in midair, out of Jason's reach.

"I am also copying selected passages from the anti-Nicene fathers," Brother Petros added, releasing his hand from the doorknob. He took a few steps toward Jason. "I would like to have you visit me sometime. My cell is only three doors down. Do you think you could come?"

"Yes."

"Tonight perhaps, before midnight prayers?"

"Of course."

"Then I shall expect you. If you want, we can chant together."

He was gone, his surging weight still quivering in the cell. Feeling a sudden chill, Jason threw more coals into the brazier and once again picked up the pages of music. He did not get very far. With the first strains of David's psalm, Danae came dancing into his heart.

5

A peculiar odor met his nostrils when he entered the cell of Brother Petros later that night. The room was unkempt. Articles of clothing were tossed on the floor next to the bed; a small table was cluttered with books and sundry items; an icon of Saint Peter hung askew on the wall above the bed. The brazier glowed with heat but the kerosene lamp kept spitting and was almost out.

Brother Petros was overjoyed to see him. He brushed away the books that were on a folding chair and asked him to sit. "Do you want to chant now?"

"Any time you say," replied Jason.

The monk sat on the edge of his bed and closed his eyes for a moment. "Let us try the Fourth Plagian Mode. It is my favorite. Here, I have the notes written down in this small book." He gave Jason a pitch. "Is this too low for you?"

"I do not think so."

"The words are from David's forty-second psalm. Hold the book under the lamp and follow me."

"I think the lamp needs more oil," said Jason.

Brother Petros filled the lamp with kerosene then came quickly back to the bed. His voice was robust and lacked the sensitive elegance of Brother Antonios'. Jason tried to keep up with him but the monk kept barreling ahead, entranced by the sound of his own words. When they reached the end of the psalm, he rubbed his hands vigorously and said to Jason, "You did well. It is incredible how rapidly you have mastered the chant!"

For the first time, Jason observed the man's rough hands. They seemed out of place here. "How long have you been a monk?" he asked.

"Only two years," said Brother Petros. "I used to work as a stevedore on the docks of Kalamata."

"What brought you to the monastery?"

"It was my father's doing. 'Is this to be your life,' he kept ranting at me, 'carrying those heavy bags on your shoulder like a beast of burden?' As the first chanter in Sparta, he knew everything about religious matters. He also perceived that I had no real interest in marriage. One day he brought me up here for a visit but I liked it so much I decided to stay."

They chanted from Isaiah. This time Brother Petros proceeded at a slower pace and Jason was able to stay with him. After an hour he got up from the chair.

"Where are you going?" asked Brother Petros.

"I must go back to my cell."

"But why?"

"Brother Antonios will be expecting me."

The monk looked hurt. "Please stay. I have something to show you." Reaching under the bed, he pulled out a bulky object covered in burlap. Fleetingly, Jason noticed that it was stuffed with straw: a crudely devised figure with limbs hanging loosely from both sides, head drooping above two uneven lumps on the chest.

He held it in front of Jason and whispered hoarsely, "Here, we can share her together, but you must not tell anyone!"

Jason scurried for the door but Brother Petros leaped forward and thrust the manikin into his arms. He was repelled by the odor. It was the same smell that struck him when he first entered the cell. Angrily he flung it to the floor and kicked it several times until the senseless head flew off. Another kick sent the arms and legs flying. He lost his balance and almost fell but he kept on kicking the thing until it finally split open, hurling a cloud of straw over the room.

Brother Petros dropped to his knees and desperately tried to gather all the broken parts, sweeping the straw and burlap into his arms, wringing his head in agony. "You killed her! You killed her!"

Jason felt a plague of nausea as he reached for the doorknob. He flung the door open but before he could stagger out of the cell something struck him on the back of the head. He leaned against the door, weak and dazed, sinking. Another blow infested his brain with darkness.

• •

He was lying face-down on the bed, naked, his arms and legs tied to the metal posts with heavy rope, a wad of cloth stuffed into his mouth. He strained to free himself, tugging violently at the rope, tearing his skin. Over his shoulder, a thunderous voice quaked: "Have mercy upon me, oh Lord, according to Thy loving kindness, according to the multitude of Thy tender mercies blot out my transgression . . ."

Viselike fingers dug into his flesh, running along his neck and back. He felt the crunching weight of a body, a voice thick with lust: "Against Thee have I sinned and done this evil in Thy sight. Behold, I was shapen in iniquity; in sin did my mother conceive me . . ."

Contemptible hands, foul breath, a vile beast wedged between his buttocks!

"Purge me with hyssop and I shall be clean. Wash me and I shall be whiter than the snow . . ."

He kicked, clawed at the mattress, tried to roll to the side, but it was too late. The pernicious tumor had already burst open, sending its heinous venom over his burning body.

6

He awoke under a veil of shadows. Through the pale window-panes he could discern snowflakes falling. He was burning with fever and shame. Horrible spasms racked his body. Turning his head, he saw Brother Timotheos leaning over the bed. With him were Brother Antonios, Father Athanasios, and Brother Eugenios the hospitaler of the monastery. Brother Timotheos kept whispering, "Be strong, my son. The ordeal is over."

Brother Antonios, hands clenched, was trembling. "I came to your cell, Jason, but you were not there. I could hear strange sounds coming from that animal's cell when I stepped out into the balcony. I pushed the door open and saw what he was doing to you. I picked up your heavy cane from the floor and struck him on the head. May God forgive me, I struck him many times!"

Jason fastened his eyes on the falling snow.

"I killed him, Jason. I killed him!"

The abbot begged Brother Antonios to calm himself. Coming closer to Jason, he whispered, "From the day Brother Petros arrived here, he was a thorn in our flesh. I should have taken the time to observe him more vigilantly. Several monks complained about his busy hands, his overbearing efforts to befriend everyone, but I chided them and warned that they should close their eyes to such evil thoughts and regard Brother Petros with love and kindness."

Brother Antonios slid to his knees and began beating his breast. The abbot commanded him to stop but the monk kept at it until the hospitaler lifted him to his feet and escorted him gently out of the room. A few moments later, the abbot left. In the dull silence, Jason felt Brother Timotheos' hand on his brow.

•   •

The abbot left strict orders with the hospitaler that Jason remain in the infirmary until he was fully recovered. Brother Timotheos came daily to visit him but Jason had no desire to speak with him. Brother Antonios never appeared. When Jason was finally released from the infirmary, Brother Timotheos walked with him across the quadrangle and up the stairs to his cell. Jason was in no mood for conversation but he softened when he saw the hurt look on Brother Timotheos' face.

"I must tell you about Brother Antonios," said the old monk. "He is not well."

"What ails him?"

"He is confined to the upper room of the infirmary. No one is permitted to see him."

"Is he seriously ill?"

"His mind has become unstable. He really believes that he killed that evil man."

"He did not kill him?"

"No. He rendered him unconscious and as soon as the evil one came to his senses Father Athanasios expelled him from the monastery."

Jason picked up his cane from the bed and started for the door.

"Where are you going?" said Brother Timotheos with alarm.

Jason did not answer.

"But you cannot see him. Father Athanasios forbids it!"

In the quadrangle, Jason brushed against the branch of a fruit tree, frightening the white birds and causing them to escape deeper into the branches. The monastery was quiet. No one saw him enter the infirmary. The hospitaler's door was wide open but he was not inside. Jason climbed the stairs to the upper room and found the door locked. He came downstairs and released the key from behind the door of a vacant room and tried it on the door upstairs. It opened.

The shades were drawn. The bed was empty. In the far corner on the floor, Brother Antonios sat cross-legged, lips murmuring, eyes riveted to the bare wall.

Jason spoke his name but there was no response. He moved across the room and touched the monk on the shoulder. Nothing. The eyes were still detached, the lips kept murmuring.

"Brother Antonios, look at me."

He was speaking to the wind.

Dejectedly he walked back to the door then stopped. Hating himself and feeling very ill at ease, he began chanting:

Lord, I cry unto Thee,
Make haste;
Give ear unto my voice
When I cry unto Thee . . .

The lips stopped murmuring.

Make haste;
Give ear unto my voice
When I cry unto Thee!

Slowly the eyes turned away from the bare wall—the curtain opening, the daze and confusion melting away, the recognition.

Attend unto my cry;
Bring my soul out of prison,
That I may praise Thy name . . .

Brother Antonios was reaching out to him. Jason hurried across the room and pulled the monk to his feet. The delicate arms embraced him without words or tears.

Just then, Jason turned around and saw Brother Timotheos standing beside the open door, weeping and crossing himself.

•   •

The next morning he walked alone to the windlass. Stepping to the edge of the summit, he glared at his cane for a long while and then hurled it into the air. It made a sharp echo when it landed on the rocks below. He did not stumble even once all the way back to the quadrangle. Brother Timotheos had just stepped out of the refectory.

"I am delighted to see you, my son. What happened to your cane?"

"I do not need it any longer."

"Brother Eugenios cooked us an excellent pea soup."

"I have decided to leave the monastery," said Jason.

"When?"

"Tomorrow morning."

"I think you should wait for another week or so. Boreas is treacherous this time of year."

"I have made up my mind," said Jason.

Brother Timotheos hunched his shoulders. "Is there anything I can do for you?"

"I need some clothes—a pair of trousers, a shirt."

Brother Timotheos nodded. "I think I can find some in the laundry but they may not fit you."

"I will wear anything."

Brother Timotheos walked with him as far as the staircase. "Are you going back to your village, my son?"

"I do not know."

"Do you have other plans?"

"No."

The old monk reached into his cassock pocket and took out a small gold cross. "Here, I want you to have this."

Jason refused to take it.

"You must," insisted Brother Timotheos. "It will be a tender memory of the wonderful days we spent here together." He placed the cross in Jason's hand and folded his fingers over it. Jason tried to give it back but Brother Timotheos started to walk away. "I will go to the laundry right now and look for some clothes. It should not take me long."

Alone in his cell, Jason paced back and forth then waited by the window. His fingers went to the gold cross in his trouser pocket. He withdrew it and held it against the light of the window. It was coated with age. He sighed bitterly. A tarnished old cross and a bucket of bones in a cell, this was the entire estate of Brother Timotheos.

7

More snow on the mountain. Jason had to get up several times during the night to put coals in the brazier. The savage breath of Boreas had coated the cell window. He could not go back to sleep. At daybreak he unwrapped the bundle of clothes that Brother Timotheos had brought him. He felt strangely comfortable when he put the shirt and sweater on. The trousers were several sizes too large and he had to tie the waist with strong twine. He picked up his uniform from the chair and tore it to shreds, first the trousers then the shirt and coat. He held each piece over the brazier until the flames consumed it. Smoke filled the cell, dragging his mind over the railroad tracks to Monastir, Koritsa, Argyrokastron, Dukat.

It was time to leave.

He bade farewell to the abbot and shifted his feet uneasily when Father Athanasios blessed him and spoke for the final time about a world of peace and love. Brother Antonios was waiting for him outside the abbot's quarters. Tearfully, he explained to Jason that he wanted to accompany him to the summit but Brother Eugenios did not think it would be wise, exerting himself through the heavy drifts of snow. Jason accepted his embrace and slowly walked away.

Brother Timotheos remained at his side, begging Jason to postpone his departure, warning him once again about the wind, the driving snow. But Jason was determined. When they reached the wooden bridge, which was now obliterated by snow, the wind increased its velocity. Brother Timotheos again tried to dissuade him but Jason attached his thoughts to the four rope pullers who were breaking a path to the summit.

The wind struck them even more furiously when they reached the windlass. The straw cage and coil of rope were completely covered with snow and the four monks had to labor for a long time, sweeping it away. They tested the floor of the cage, the center post that held the roof, and the strong bolt to which the rope was secured. After this, they went over every inch of the rope, making certain it was not frayed or worn.

"My son, I implore you to wait until another day," said Brother Timotheos.

Jason walked to the cage. One of the monks checked the door and made sure it was latched tightly after Jason stepped in. Sorrowfully, Brother Timotheos lifted his hand and blessed him. He blessed the cage, the rope, the windlass, the four monks, the raging wind and snow. By this time the cage had been dragged to the very edge of the precipice.

The four monks took a firm hold on the rope and started guiding it slowly over the windlass. In the next instant, the cage was hanging in the air, spinning wildly, a pawn in the hands of the wind. It hung there for a long moment before it finally began to drop. Soon Brother Timotheos disappeared from view, his last blessing swallowed by wind and snow. As the cage fell swiftly, Jason could sense Pavlo's wrath swarming over him: *You are a deplorable sight, friend Jason. Look at yourself, trapped in that silly cage, dressed in those baggy clothes. You look like the idiot Fanoulis. If only you had listened to me, we would both be in America today!*

Jason could see nothing but bare precipice. The earth was rushing up to meet him. In a moment of despair, he wished that he could remain in this state forever, suspended between two worlds, never allowing anyone or anything to touch him, riding the wings of the wind.

The cage started to swing away from the precipice in wide angles. A demented wind had grabbed hold of it and was throwing it out into hostile space, stretching the rope as far as it could reach. Suddenly the wind veered and the cage hurtled back toward the precipice. The blow knocked him to the floor but he kept his hold on the strong center post.

He braced himself for the second blow. The third. Parts of the straw walls broke off, and again the cage was blown away into a foreign sky, only to return once more, screeching and crashing into the hard ribs of the precipice. The blows were relentless, shattering most of the cage, knocking away half the floor, but miraculously the center post remained unharmed, its strong arm still clutching the iron ring that held the rope.

His grandfather's finger touched his head: '*My little Icarus, you will never fly unless you learn to free yourself of the earth's pull. Let go and free yourself!*'

The cage kept plummeting downward, turning and swerving, bouncing against the precipice, a leaf in a storm.

Bitterly, he laughed at himself: *Jason, bell-ringer of Saint Chrysostomos, it will be over soon. No one will know that you ever existed. The jackals and wolves will devour your flesh and bones. Your name will be lost in oblivion!*

There was a pocket of calm.

Much of the wind's anger abated as it kept flinging the cage against the precipice, but they were glancing blows, tired thrusts of a spent titan.

Jason felt a sudden thump under his feet. The cage hurdled over a snow-covered ridge, bouncing many times before it finally came to a stop. He released his hold on the post and fell headlong into a blinding world of white. He could not move. Lying on his back, he lifted his eyes and saw the crippled cage retreating into the sky, losing itself in a glare of light.

When at last he was able to get on his feet, he searched for an opening in the high drifts of snow but could not find one. Struggling through the snow, he almost fell down and in one terrifying instant wished that he had his cane. He cursed himself then scooped up some snow and tossed it over his face. His heart could not stop pounding. After a while his eyes became more accustomed to the strong light and he decided to plow his way through the first drift. The effort drained him and he was tempted to lie down again.

By mid-morning he had made some progress, reaching the stony heights of a perilous cliff. The baggy trousers were heavy with wet snow; his leg ached.

From the top of the cliff he caught a glimpse of Akra. He kept climbing until he approached a craggy summit. Swinging around its slippery rocks, he found a narrow slit and worked his way through it, coming eventually before a long slope. The drifts were not as deep here and he managed to descend more rapidly. Within an hour he was entirely free of snow and wind.

It was spring in Akra.

The first poppies had already opened; birds were flying over the village with grace and joy. Barba Yianni answered his loud knock on the door. At first the old man did not recognize him but when Jason came closer Barba Yianni tearfully embraced him. "You are not wearing your uniform," he exclaimed. "Where is your cane?"

"I do not need it anymore," said Jason.

Barba Yianni ambled to a closet and brought out a bottle of ouzo. "This will perk you up, my son. You look pale and worn." He poured some ouzo into a glass and watched Jason gulp it down. Jason asked for another and the old man eagerly filled the glass again.

Feeling drowsy, Jason leaned back in the chair and closed his eyes. When he awoke there was an aroma of roasting meat in the cottage. Lamb and dandelions. It was the first time he had eaten anything substantial since Ioannina. He devoured many slices of the bread that had the earth's scent in it.

Just before dusk Barba Yianni started to prepare another bed but Jason stopped him. "I cannot stay," he said.

"But it is getting late, my son. Sleep here tonight and you can depart tomorrow."

"No, I must leave now."

"Where are you going?"

"To my village, Livani."

"But I thought you had no desire to go back there."

"I cannot explain it now. There is no time."

"My son, Livani is several hours from here. You are tired. I beg you, stay the night in my cottage . . ."

Jason shook his head. He thanked the old man for the ouzo and for the meal. Before opening the kitchen door, he said, "Did Kitso come back safely?"

"Who?"

"Your donkey, Kitso."

"Ah, yes. He took you to the monastery that morning. Of course he came back. Where else could he have gone?"

Barba Yianni offered his hand to him but Jason swept him into his arms and held him tightly. Like Greece, he was skin and bone.

"Goodbye, my son. May Saint Andrew protect you. May you have a joyful reunion with your family and friends in Livani."

"Perhaps we will meet again," said Jason.

Barba Yianni crossed himself. "God willing, my son. God willing."

He came all the way to the street with Jason then embraced him once again. "A Good Hour to you, my son. I hope you reach your village before darkness sets in."

Jason kept waving to him until he and Akra were lost from view. He had to fight for almost two hours before he could defeat the last slope at the entrance to the north pass. He sat down to rest. Livani lay sprawled out below him. He could almost reach out and touch the quay, the square, the church. He envisioned the children at play in the schoolyard, the women baking in the ovens, the old men sitting in the taverna.

His heart cried out for Danae.

He dreaded the thought of facing Yianoula and little Renio. What could he say to them? Pavlo was no help: *Behold, you are returning to the labyrinth, friend Jason, tail between your legs, like a dog going back to its own vomit. You had your chance, your one great chance, but no, you refused to take it!*

It was dark when he approached the village. Several figures were moving about in the square. He could not make them out. He wondered who would be the first to greet him. How would he respond? He felt as though he had been away for an eternity.

There were no lights in the taverna. Every house was in darkness. Momentarily, he was confused. This did not seem like Livani. The dogs were not barking. The church looked desolate and cold.

Again his thoughts raced to Danae.

He could not wait to look into her face, take her into his arms. But first he had to go to his aunt Yianoula and tell her about the money in the cellar, about Pavlo's last wish that they all go to America: Yianoula and Renio, his mother and father, Danae. He and Danae would raise their children in America; name their first boy Pavlo . . .

Coming into the heart of the square, he tried to peer through the darkness. The shadowy figures were lifting heavy boxes and piling them against the trunk of the plane tree. He ran forward to meet them but stopped abruptly when he noticed their strange uniforms; heard their strange voices. Something warned him to turn around, flee into the mountains and hide there until the village lights burned brightly again, until the church bell rang and the dogs barked.

It was too late.

The uniforms had already moved away from the pile of boxes and were edging toward him. His eyes darted around the square then froze on the lorry: on its side panel, against a stark white circle, loomed the jagged claw of the German swastika.